A STARTLING TRANSFORMATION

Enchanting, golden-haired Cleone Charteris was just on the eve of her London debut. From her family's country house she yearned for the gaiety, the glamour, the style of the great fashionable world.

Small wonder that when the elegant, impeccable Mr. Bancroft came down from the city, Cleone's head was turned. Even though she had always loved Philip Jettan—strong, handsome, countrified Philip! Surely, if he loved her, he would allow himself to be reformed into a suave man of the world!

Only when Philip took this project into his own hands and returned from Paris transformed beyond Bancroft's wildest excesses of fashion, did Cleone realize her awful mistake . . .

POWDER AND PATCH

A high-spirited comedy of manners, young love, and the dictates of 18th-century fashion.

Bantam Books by Georgette Heyer
Ask your bookseller for the books you have missed

Historical Romances

THE CORINTHIAN
THESE OLD SHADES
DEVIL'S CUB
THE CONVENIENT MARRIAGE
REGENCY BUCK
THE CONQUEROR
BLACK SHEEP
FARO'S DAUGHTER
THE MASQUERADERS
THE TALISMAN RING
THE BLACK MOTH
THE NONESUCH
FALSE COLOURS
AN INFAMOUS ARMY
BEAUVALLET
POWDER AND PATCH
COUSIN KATE
ROYAL ESCAPE
THE SPANISH BRIDE
A BLUNT INSTRUMENT

Mysteries

WHY SHOOT A BUTLER?
THEY FOUND HIM DEAD

Soon to be published by Bantam

GEORGETTE HEYER
POWDER AND PATCH

(The Transformation of Philip Jettan)

A COMEDY OF MANNERS

BANTAM BOOKS · TORONTO · NEW YORK · LONDON
A NATIONAL GENERAL COMPANY

This low-priced Bantam Book
has been completely reset in a type face
designed for easy reading, and was printed
from new plates. It contains the complete
text of the original hard-cover edition.
NOT ONE WORD HAS BEEN OMITTED.

POWDER AND PATCH

A Bantam Book / published by arrangement with
E. P. Dutton & Company, Inc.

PRINTING HISTORY

Dutton edition published June 1968
2nd printing ... September 1968
Bantam edition published November 1969

Bantam Books are published by Bantam Books, Inc., a National
General company. Its trade-mark, consisting of the words "Bantam
Books" and the portrayal of a bantam, is registered in the United
States Patent Office and in other countries. Marca Registrada.
Bantam Books, Inc., 666 Fifth Avenue, New York, N.Y. 10019.

PRINTED IN THE UNITED STATES OF AMERICA

CONTENTS

CHAPTER I

The House of Jettan

If you searched among the Downs in Sussex, somewhere between Midhurst and Brighthelmstone, inland
a little, and nestling in modest seclusion between two
waves of hills, you would find Little Fittledean, a village round which three gentlemen had built their
homes. One chose the north side, half a mile away,
and on the slope of the Downs. He was Mr. Winton,
a dull man with no wife, but two children, James and
Jennifer. The second built his house west of the village, not far from the London Road and Great Fittledean. He was one Sir Thomas Jettan. He chose his
site carefully, beside a wood, and laid out gardens
after the Dutch style. That was way back in the last
century when Charles the Second was King, and what
had then been a glaring white erection, stark-naked
and blatant in its sylvan setting, was now, some sev-
enty years later, a fair place, creeper-hung, and made
kindly by the passing of the years. The Jettan who
built it became inordinately proud of the house.
Never a day passed but he would strut round the
grounds, looking at the nude structure from a hundred different points of vantage. It was to be the country seat of the Jettans in their old age; they were to
think of it almost as they would think of their children. It was never to be sold; it was to pass from fa-

ther to son and from son to grandson through countless ages. Nor must it accrue to a female heir, be she never so direct, for old Tom determined that the name of Jettan should always be associated with the house.

Old Tom propounded these notions to the whole countryside. All his friends and his acquaintances were shown the white house and told the tale of its owner's past misdemeanours and his present virtue—a virtue due, he assured them, to the possession of so fair an estate. No more would he pursue the butterfly existence that all his ancestors had pursued before him. This house was his anchor and his interest; he would rear his two sons to reverence it, and it might even be that the tradition which held every Jettan to be a wild fellow at heart should be broken at last.

The neighbours laughed behind their hands at old Tom's childishness. They dubbed the hitherto unnamed house "Tom's Pride", in good-humoured raillery.

Tom Jettan was busy thinking out a suitable name for his home when the countryside's nickname came to his ears. He was not without humour in spite of his vanity, and when the sobriquet had sunk into his brain, he chuckled deep in his chest, and slapped his knee in appreciation. Not a month later the neighbours were horrified to find, cunningly inserted in the wrought-iron gates of the white house, a gilded scroll bearing the legend, "Jettan's Pride". No little apprehension was felt amongst them at having their secret joke thus discovered and utilised, and those who next waited on Tom did so with an air of ashamed nervousness. But Tom soon made it clear that, far from being offended, he was grateful to them for finding an appropriate name for his home.

His hopeful prophecy concerning the breaking of tradition was not realised in either of his sons. The elder, Maurice, sowed all the wild oats of which he was capable before taking up his abode at the Pride; the other, Thomas, never ceased sowing wild oats, and showed no love for the house whatsoever.

When old Tom died he left a will which gave Maurice to understand that if, by the time he was fifty years of age, he still refused to settle down at the Pride, it was to pass to his brother and his brother's heirs.

Thomas counselled Maurice to marry and produce some children.

"For damme if I do, my boy! The old man must have lost his faculties to expect a Jettan to live in this hole! I tell ye flat, Maurice, I'll not have the place. 'Tis you who are the elder, and you must assume the —the responsibilities!" At that he fell a-chuckling, for he was an irrepressible scamp.

"Certainly I shall live here," answered Maurice. "Three months here, and nine months—not here. What's to stop me?"

"Does the will allow it?" asked Tom doubtfully.

"It does not forbid it. And I shall get me a wife."

At that Tom burst out laughing, but checked himself hurriedly as he met his brother's reproving eye.

"God save us, and the old gentleman but three days dead! Not that I meant any disrespect, y'know. Faith, the old man 'ud be the first to laugh with me, stap me if he wouldn't!" He stifled another laugh, and shrugged his shoulders. "Or he would before he went crazy-pious over this devilish great barn of a house. You'll never have the money to keep it, Maurry," he added cheerfully, "let alone a wife."

Maurice twirled his eyeglass, frowning.

"My father has left even more than I expected," he said.

"Oh ay! But it'll be gone after a week's play! God ha' mercy, Maurry, do ye hope to husband it?"

"Nay, I hope to husband a wife. The rest I'll leave to her."

Tom came heavily to his feet. He stared at his brother, round-eyed.

"Blister me, but I believe the place is turning you like the old gentleman! Now, Maurry, Maurry, stiffen your back, man!"

Maurice smiled.

"It'll take more than the Pride to reform me, Tom. I'm thinking that the place is too good to sell or throw away."

"If I could lay my hand on two thousand guineas," said Tom, "anyone could have the Pride for me!"

Maurice looked up quickly.

"Why, Tom, all I've got's yours, you know very well! Take what you want—two thousand or twenty."

"Devilish good of you, Maurry, but I'll not sponge on you yet. No, don't start to argue with me, for my head's not strong enough what with one thing and another. Tell me more of this wife of yours. Who is it to be?"

"I haven't decided," replied Maurice. He yawned slightly. "There are so many to choose from."

"Ay—you're an attractive devil—'pon my word you are! What d'ye say to Lucy Farmer?"

Maurice shuddered.

"Spare me. I had thought of Marianne Tempest."

"What, old Castlehill's daughter? She'd kill you in a month, lad."

"But she is not—dowerless."

4

"No. But think of it, Maurry! Think of it! A shrew at twenty!"

"Then what do you think of Jane Butterfield?"

Thomas pulled at his lip, irresolute.

"I'm not decrying the girl, Maurice, but Lord! could you live with her?"

"I've not essayed it," answered Maurice.

"No, and marriage is so damned final! 'Tisn't as though ye could live together for a month or so before ye made up your minds. I doubt the girl would not consent to that."

"And if she did consent, one would not desire to wed her," remarked Maurice. "A pity. No, I believe I could not live with Jane."

Thomas sat down again.

"The truth of it is, Maurry, we Jettans must marry for love. There's not one of us ever married without it, whether for money or no."

"'Tis so unfashionable," objected Maurice. "One marries for convenience. One may have fifty different loves."

"What! All at once? I think you'd find that a trifle inconvenient, Maurry! Lord! just fancy fifty loves—oh, the devil! And three's enough to drive one crazed, bruise me if 'tis not."

Maurice's thin lips twitched responsively.

"Gad no! Fifty loves spread over a lifetime, and you're not bound to one of them. There's bliss, Tom, you rogue!"

Thomas shook a wise finger at him, his plump, good-humoured face solemn all at once.

"And not one of them's the true love, Maurry. For if she were, faith, she'd not be one of fifty! Now, you take my advice, lad, and wait. Damme, we'll not spoil the family record!"

A rakish youth, says the Jettan adage,
Marriage for love, and a staid old age.

"I don't know that it's true about the staid old age,
though. Maybe 'tis only those who wed for love who
acquire virtue. Anyway, you'll not break the second
maxim, Maurry."

"Oh?" smiled Maurice. "What's to prevent me?"

Thomas had risen again. Now he slipped his arm in
his brother's.

"If it comes to prevention, old sobersides, I'm game.
I'll make an uproar in the church and carry off the
bride. Gad, but 'twould be amusing! Carry off one's
brother's bride, under his stern nose. Devil take it,
Maurry, that's just what your nose is! I never thought
on't before—stern, grim, old—now, steady, Tom, my
boy, or you'll be laughing again with the old gentleman not yet under ground!"

Maurice waited for his brother's mirth to abate.

"But, Tom, 'tis very well for you to counsel me not
to wed without love! I must marry, for 'tis certain
you'll not, and we must have heirs. What's to be done,
I'd like to know?"

"Wait, lad, wait! You're not so old that you can't
afford to hold back yet awhile."

"I'm thirty-five, Tom."

"Then you have fifteen years to run before you
need settle down. Take my advice, and wait!"

The end of it was that Maurice did wait. For four
years he continued to rove through Europe, amusing
himself in the usual way of gentlemen of his day, but
in 1729 he wrote a long letter from Paris to his
brother in London, declaring himself in love, and the
lady an angel of goodness, sweetness, amiability, and
affection. He said much more in this vein, all of

6

which Tom had to read, yawning and chuckling by turns. The lady was one Maria Marchant. She brought with her a fair dowry and a placid disposition. So Tom wrote off to Maurice at once, congratulating him, and bestowing his blessing on the alliance. He desired his dear old Maurry to quit travelling, and to come home to his affectionate brother Tom.

In a postscript he added that he dropped five hundred guineas at Newmarket, only to win fifteen hundred at dice the very next week, so that had it not been for his plaguey ill-luck in the matter of a small wager with Harry Besham, he would to-day be the most care-free of mortals, instead of a jaded creature, creeping about in terror of the bailiffs from hour to hour.

After that there was no more correspondence. Neither brother felt that there was anything further to be said, and they were not men to waste their time writing to one another for no urgent matter. Thomas thought very little more about Maurice's marriage. He supposed that the wedding would take place in England before many months had gone by; possibly Maurice would see fit to return at once, as he, Tom, had suggested. In the meantime, there was nothing to be done. Tom laid his brother's letter aside, and went on with his ordinary occupations.

He lived in Half-Moon Street. His house was ruled by his cook, the wife of Moggat, his valet-footman. She also ruled the hapless Moggat. Moggat retaliated by ruling his jovial master as far as he was able, so one might really say Mrs. Moggat ruled them all. As Tom was quite unaware of this fact, it troubled him not a whit.

A month after he had answered his brother's letter, Tom was disturbed one morning while he sipped his chocolate with the news that a gentleman wished to speak to him. Tom was in his bedchamber, his round person swathed in a silken wrapper of astonishing brightness. He had not yet doffed his nightcap, and his wig lay on the dressing-table.

The lean, long Moggat crept in at the door, which he seemed hardly to open, and ahem'd directly behind his master.

Tom was in the act of swallowing his chocolate, and he had not heard Moggat's slithering approach, the violent clearing of that worthy's throat startled him not a little, and he choked.

Tenderly solicitous, Moggat patted him on the back until the coughs and splutters had abated. Tom bounced round in his chair to face the man.

"Damn and curse it, Moggat! What d'ye mean by it? What d'ye mean by it, I say? Crawling into a room to make a noise at me just as I'm drinking! Yes, sir! Just as I'm drinking! Devil take you! D'ye hear me? Devil take you!"

Moggat listened in mournful silence. When Tom ceased for want of breath, he bowed, and continued as though there had been no interruption.

"There is a gentleman below, sir, as desires to have speech with you."

"A gentleman? Don't you know that gentlemen don't come calling at this hour, ye ninny-pated jackass? Bring me some more chocolate!"

"Yes, sir, a gentleman."

"I tell you no gentleman would disturb another at this hour! Have done now, Moggat!"

"And although I told the gentleman, sir, as how my master was not yet robed and accordingly could not see any visitors, he said it was of no consequence to him whatsoever, and he would be obliged to you to ask him upstairs at once, sir. So I—"

"Confound his impudence!" growled Tom. "What's his name?"

"The gentleman, sir, on my asking what name I was to tell you, gave me to understand that it was of no matter."

"Devil take him! Show him out, Moggat! Like as not 'tis one of these cursed bailiffs. Why, you fool, what d'ye mean by letting him in?"

Moggat sighed in patient resignation.

"If you will allow me to say so, sir, this gentleman is not a bailiff."

"Well, who is he?"

"I regret, sir, I do not know."

"You're a fool! What's this fellow like?"

"The gentleman"—Moggat laid ever so little stress on the word—"is tall, sir, and—er—slim. He is somewhat dark as regards eyes and brows, and he is dressed, if I may say so, exceedingly modishly, with a point-edged hat, and very full-skirted puce coat, laced, French fashion, with—"

Tom snatched his nightcap off and threw it at Moggat.

"Numskull! D'ye think I want a list of his clothes? Show him out, the swarthy rogue! Show him out!"

Moggat picked up the nightcap, and smoothed it sadly.

"The gentleman seems anxious to see you, sir."

"Ay! Trying to dun me, the rascal! Don't I know it! Blustering and—"

"No, sir," said Moggat firmly. "I could not truthfully say that the gentleman blustered. Indeed, sir, if I may say so, I think him a singularly quiet, cool gentleman. Very soft-spoken, sir—oh, very soft-spoken!"

"Take him away!" shouted Tom. "I tell you I'll not be pestered at this hour! I might be asleep, damme! Tell the fellow to come again at a godly time—not at dawn! Now, don't try to argue, Moggat! I tell you, if it were my brother himself, I'd not see him!"

Moggat bowed again.

"I will hinform the gentleman, sir."

When the door closed behind Moggat, Tom leant back in his chair and picked up one of his letters. Not five minutes later the door creaked again. Tom turned, to find Moggat at his elbow.

"Eh? What d'ye want?"

"Hif you please, sir, the gentleman says as how he is your brother," said Moggat gently.

Tom jumped as though he had been shot.

"What? My brother? What d'ye mean? My brother?"

"Sir Maurice, sir."

Up flew Tom, catching at his wig and cramming it on his head all awry.

"Thunder an' turf! Maurry! Here, you raving wooden-pate! How dare you leave my brother downstairs? How dare you, I say?" He wrapped himself more tightly in his robe than ever, and dashed headlong out of the room, down the stairs to where Maurice awaited him.

Sir Maurice was standing by the window in the library, drumming his fingers on the sill. At his brother's tempestuous entrance he turned and bowed.

"A nice welcome you give me, Tom! 'Tell him to come again at a godly time—I'd not see him if 'twere my brother himself,' forsooth!"

Thomas hopped across the room and seized both Maurice's long, thin hands in his plump, chubby ones.

"My dear Maurry! My dear old fellow! I'd no notion 'twas you! My dolt of a lackey—but there! When did you arrive in England?"

"A week ago. I have been at the Pride."

"A week? What a plague d'ye mean by not coming to me till now, ye rogue?" As he spoke, Tom thrust Maurice into a chair, and himself sat down opposite him, beaming with pleasure.

Maurice leant back, crossing his legs. A little smile flickered across his mouth, but his eyes were solemn as he answered:

"I had first to see my wife installed in her new home," he said.

For a moment Tom stared at him.

"Wife? Tare an' 'ouns, ye don't waste your time! Where and when did you marry the lady?"

"Three weeks ago, at Paris. Now I have come home to fulfil the last part of the Jettan adage."

"God ha' mercy!" ejaculated Thomas. "Not a staid old age, lad! Not you?"

"Something like it," nodded Maurice. "Wait till you have seen my wife!"

"Ay, I'm waiting," said Tom. "What's to do now, then? The country squire, and half a dozen children?"

The grey eyes twinkled.

"Tom, I'll thank you not to be so coarse."

"Coarse? *Coarse?* Gad, Maurice, what's come over you?"

"I am a married man," replied Maurice. "As such I have—er—learnt to guard my tongue. My wife—"

"Maurry, couldn't ye call the lady by her name?" begged Tom. "Faith, I can't bear those two words so often, proud though ye may be of them."

Maurice flushed slightly and smiled.

"Maria, then. She is a very—sweet, delicate lady."

"Lord! I'd made up my mind you'd wed a bold, strapping wench with a saucy smile, Maurry!"

"I? Good God, no! My w— Maria is gentle, and meek, and—"

"Ay, ay, Maurry, I know!" hastily interrupted Thomas. "I must see her for myself, so don't spoil the surprise for me, there's a good fellow! Now have you breakfasted? No? Then come upstairs with me. Where's that rascal Moggat? Moggat! Moggat! Ah, there you are! Go and prepare breakfast at once, man! And bring some more chocolate to my room." He wrapped the voluminous robe about him once more, and, seizing his brother by the arm, led him forth to the staircase.

Thus it was that Maurice Jettan brought home his bride. She was a gentle lady, with a sweet disposition; she adored her handsome husband, and duly presented him with a son, Philip. When the babe was shown to him, Tom discovered that he was a true Jettan, with all their characteristics. His father confessed that he saw no resemblance either to himself or to anyone, but he was nevertheless gratified by his brother's remarks. Tom chuckled mightily and prophesied that young Philip would prove himself a Jettan in more ways than one. He hinted at a youth which should surpass his father's in brilliancy, and Maurice smiled, looking proudly down at the red, crumpled face.

"And," concluded Tom, "he'll have a papa who can advise him in all matters of fashion better than any man I know. Why, Maurice, you will show him the fashionable world! You must take care you do not stagnate here. You must not fall out of Society."

Maurice was still smiling down at his offspring.

"No. I must not fall out, Tom. The youngster will need me later on."

For five years he continued to take his place in London Society, but he found that the desire for excitement and gaiety was growing less and less within him. The death of Maria gave this desire the *coup de grâce*. Maurice took his small son down to the Pride as soon as he had recovered from the first shock of bereavement, and after that for some years he rarely visited London, except sometimes to see his brother or his tailor. Then he seemed to grow restless again, and started to spend more time with Tom. Bit by bit he re-entered the world he had quitted, yet never did he give himself up to it as once he had done. The Pride seemed to call him, and little Philip held his heart with both hands. Thereafter he spent his time between London and the Pride. When he felt restless, he packed his bags and flitted either to London or to Paris; when the restlessness had passed, back he came to the Pride, there to spend two or three peaceful months.

When Philip was eighteen, he took him to London. Philip was thoroughly bored. Sir Maurice concluded that he was too young to be introduced into Society, and he sent him back to the country, thinking that in two or three years' time the lad would be only too anxious to leave it.

But the years slipped by, and Philip showed no desire to follow in his father's footsteps. He refused to go on the Grand Tour; he cared nothing for Dress or

Fashionable Manners; he despised the life of Courts; he preferred to remain in the country, usurping, to a great extent, his father's position as squire. He was now some twenty-three years old, tall and handsome, but, as his father told his uncle, "an unpolished cub."

CHAPTER II

In which is Presented Mistress Cleone Charteris

A while back I spoke of three gentlemen who built their homes round Little Fitteldean. Of one I said but little, of the second I spoke at length and to the tune of one whole chapter. It now behoves me to mention the third gentleman, who chose his site on the outskirts of the village, some two miles from Jettan's Pride, and to the east. To reach it you must walk along the main street until the cottages grow sparse and yet more sparse, and the cobblestones and pavement cease altogether. The street turns then into a lane with trees flanking it and grass growing to the sides. A few steps further, and the moss-covered roof of Sharley House peeps above a high holly hedge which screens the place from the passer-by.

There lived Mr. Charteris, and his father and grandfather before him. Mr. Charteris was the happy possessor of a wife and a daughter. It is with the daughter that I am most concerned.

Her name was Cleone, and she was very lovely. She had thick gold curls, eyes of cornflower blue, and a pair of red lips that pouted or smiled in equal fascination. She was just eighteen, and the joy and despair of all the young men of the countryside. Particularly was she the despair of Mr. Philip Jettan.

Philip was head over ears in love with Cleone. He

had been so ever since she returned from the convent where she had received a slight education. Before her departure for this convent, she and Philip, James and Jennifer Winton, had played together and quarrelled together since any of them could walk. Then Cleone went away to acquire polish, and the two boys thought very little more about her, until she returned, and then they thought of nothing else but her. The romping playfellow was gone for ever, but in her place was a Vision. Philip and James began to eye one another askance.

Delighted by the new state of affairs, Cleone queened it right royally, and played one young man against the other. But it was not long before she found herself thinking far more about Mr. Jettan than was seemly. He began to haunt her dreams, and when he came to visit the house her heart fluttered a little and showed a tendency to jump into her throat.

Cleone was stern with her heart, for there was much in Mr. Jettan that did not meet with her approval. However masterful and handsome he might be—and Philip was both—he was distressingly boorish in many ways. Before her return to Sharley House Cleone had spent a few months with her aunt, who lived in Town. Several men had made very elegant love to her and showered compliments about her golden head. She had not cared the snap of her fingers for any one of them, but their graceful homage was very gratifying. Philip's speech was direct and purposeful, and his compliments were never neat. His clothes also left much to be desired. Cleone had an eye for colour and style; she liked her cavaliers to be *à la mode*. Sir Matthew Trelawney, for instance, had affected the most wonderful stockings, clocked with butterflies; Frederick King wore so excellently fitting a coat that, it was said, he required three men to ease him into it. Philip's coat was made for comfort; he would have scorned the stockings of Matthew Trelawney. He even refused to buy a wig, but wore his own brown hair brushed back from his face and tied loosely at his neck with a piece of black ribbon. No powder, no curls, unpolished nails, and unpainted face—guiltless, too, of even the smallest patch—it was, thought Cleone, enough to make one weep. Nevertheless, she did not weep, because, for one thing it would have made her eyes red, and another, it would be of very little use. Philip must be reformed, since she— well, since she did not dislike him.

At the present time Philip had just returned from Town, whither he had been sent by his father, ostensibly to transact some business concerning the estate, but really that his unfashionable soul might succumb to the delights of Town. Philip was not aware of this secret purpose, but Cleone knew all about it. She was very fond of Sir Maurice, and he of her. When Sir Maurice saw which way Philip looked for a wife, he was pleased enough, although a Jettan might have cast his eyes much higher. But Sir Maurice, mindful of the old adage, was content to let things run their course. All that worried him was the apparent obduracy of his son in the matter of the first prophecy. He loved Philip, he did not wish to lose him, he liked his companionship, but—"By God, sir, you are a damned dull dog!"

At that young Philip's straight brows drew close over the bridge of his nose, only to relax again as he smiled.

"Well, sir, I hold two gay dogs in the family to be enough."

Sir Maurice's mouth quivered responsively.

"What's that, Philip? Do you seek to reprove me?"

"Not a whit, sir. You are you, but I—am I."

"So it seems," said his father. "And you being yourself have fallen in love with a mighty pretty child; still being yourself, you are like to be left disconsolate."

Philip had flushed slightly at the reference to Cleone. The end of the sentence left him frowning.

"What mean you, sir?"

The shrewd grey eyes, so like his own, regarded him pityingly.

"Little Mistress Cleone will have none of you an you fail to mend your ways, my son. Do you not know it? What has that dainty piece to do with a raw clodhopper like yourself?"

Philip answered low.

"If Mistress Cleone gives me her love it will be for me as I am. She is worthy a man, not a powdered, ruffled beau."

"A man! *Sacré tonnerre*, 'tis what you are, *hein?* Philip, child, get you to Town to your uncle and buy a wig."

"No, sir, I thank you. I shall do very well without a wig."

Sir Maurice drove his cane downwards at the floor in exasperation.

"*Mille diables!* You'll to Town as I say, defiant boy! You may finish the business with that scoundrel Jenkins while you are about it!"

Philip nodded.

"That I will do, sir, since you wish it."

"Bah!" retorted his father.

He had gone; now he had come back, the business details settled to his satisfaction, but with no wig. Sir

Maurice was pleased to see him again, more pleased than he appeared, as Philip was well aware. He listened to what his son had to tell him of Tom Jettan, failed to glean any of the latest society gossip, and dismissed Philip from his presence.

Half an hour later Philip rode in at the gates of Sharley House, sitting straight in his saddle, a pulse in his throat throbbing in anticipation.

Cleone saw him coming. She was seated in the parlour window, embroidering in a languid fashion. Truth to tell, she was tired of her own company and not at all averse from seeing Philip. As he passed the window she bent forward a little, smiling down at him. Philip saw her at once; indeed, he had been eyeing every window of the warm, red house in the hope that she might be sitting in one. He reined in his horse and bowed to her, hat in hand.

Cleone opened the casement wider, leaning over the sill, her golden curls falling forward under the strings of her cap.

"Why, sir, are you back already?" she asked, dimpling.

"Already!" he echoed. "It has been years! Ten years, Cleone!"

"Pooh!" she said. "Ten days—not a moment more!"

"Is that all it has seemed to you?" he said.

Cleone's cheek became faintly tinged with pink.

"What more?" she retorted. "'Tis all it is!"

Into Philip's eyes came a gleam of triumph.

"Aha! You've counted, then! Oh, Cleone!"

The roguish look fled.

"Oh!" cried Cleone, pouting. "How—how—monstrous—"

"Monstrous what, dear Cleone?"

"Impudent!" she ended. "I declare I won't see you!" As if to add weight to this statement, she shut the casement and moved away into the room.

Presently, however, she relented, and tripped downstairs to the withdrawing-room, where she found Mr. Jettan paying his respects to her mamma. She curtseyed very demurely, allowed him to kiss the tips of her fingers, and seated herself beside Madam Charteris.

Madam patted her hand.

"Well, child, here is Philip returned from Town with not a word to tell us of his gaiety!"

Cleone raised her eyes to survey Philip.

"Mamma, there is naught to tell. Philip is such a staid, sober person."

"Tut-tut!" said her mother. "Now, Philip, tell us all! Did you not meet *one* beauty to whom you lost your heart?"

"No, madam," answered Philip. "The painted society dames attract me not at all." His eyes rested on Cleone as he spoke.

"I dare say you've not yet heard the news?" Cleone said, after a slight pause. "Or did Sir Maurice tell you?"

"No—that is, I do not know. What is it? Good news?"

"It remains to be seen," she replied. "'Tis that Mr. Bancroft is to return! What think you of that?"

Philip stiffened.

"Bancroft? Sir Harold's son?"

"Yes, Henry Bancroft. Is it not exciting? Only think —he has been away nigh on eight years! Why, he must be—" she began to count on her rosy-tipped fingers "—twenty-six, or twenty-seven. Oh, a man! I do so wonder what he is like now!"

"H'm!" remarked Philip. His voice held no enthusiasm. "What does he want here?"

Cleone's long lashes fluttered down to hide the laugh in her eyes.

"To see his papa, of course. After so many years!"

Philip gave vent to a sound very like a snort.

"I'll wager there's a more potent reason! Else had he come home ere now."

"Well, I will tell you. Papa rode over to Great Fittledean two days ago, and he found Sir Harold mightily amused, did he not, Mamma?"

Madam Charteris assented vaguely. She was stitching at a length of satin, content to drop out of the conversation.

"Yes. It seems that Henry—"

"Who?" Philip straightened in his chair.

"Mr. Bancroft," said Cleone. A smile trembled on her lips. "It seems that Mr. Bancroft has had occasion to fight a duel. Is it not too dreadful?"

Philip agreed with more heartiness than he had yet shown.

"I am sure I do not know why gentlemen must fight. 'Tis very terrible, I think. But, of course, 'tis monstrous gallant and exciting. And poor Mr. Bancroft has been advised to leave London for awhile, because some great personage is angered. Papa did not say who was the gentleman he fought, but Sir Harold was vastly amused." She glanced up at Philip, in time to catch sight of the scornful frown on his face. "Oh, Philip, do *you* know? Have you perhaps heard?"

"No one who has been in Town this last week could fail to have heard," said Philip shortly. Then, very abruptly, he changed the subject.

When Philip came back to the Pride it was close on the dinner hour. He walked slowly upstairs to change his clothes, for on that point Sir Maurice was obdurate. He would not allow buckskins or riding-boots at his table. He himself was fastidious to a fault. Every evening he donned stiff satins and velvets; his thin face was painted, powdered and patched; his wig tied with great precision in the nape of his neck. He walked now with a stick, but his carriage was still fairly upright. The stick was, as Philip told him, a mere affectation.

Philip was rather silent during the first part of the meal, but when the lackeys left the room, and Sir Maurice pushed the port towards him, he spoke suddenly, as if the words had hovered on his tongue for some time.

"Father, do you hear that Bancroft is to return?"

Sir Maurice selected a nut from the dish before him, cracking it between his long, white fingers.

"I believe someone told me. What of it?"

"You said nothing of it to me."

The grey eyes lifted.

"Is he a friend of yours? I did not know."

"A friend!" Philip set his glass down with a snap. "Hardly, sir!"

"Now what's to do?" asked his father. "Why the scorn?"

"Sir, if you could but hear the gossip about him!"

"I have no doubt I should be vastly entertained," said Sir Maurice. "What's the tale?"

"The fellow is for ever embroiling himself in some low quarrel. This time it is Lady Marchand. Faugh!"

"Lady Marchand? Not Dolly Marchand?"

"I believe so. Why, sir, do you know her?"

"I—er—knew her mother. Tell me, is she as charming?"

"As I know neither her mother, nor Lady Marchand—"

Sir Maurice sighed.

"No. Of course not. Go on."

"It's a damned sordid tale, sir, and I'll spare you the details. Lord Marchand and Bancroft fought out at Ipswich. Bancroft wounded him in the lung, and 'tis said he'll not recover."

"Clumsy," remarked Sir Maurice. "So Bancroft retires?"

"The Prince of Wales is furious, as well he might be. And Bancroft brings himself and his morals here."

A faint smile hovered on Sir Maurice's lips.

"And Mr. Jettan is righteously indignant. From which I gather that Mistress Cleone is prepared to welcome this slayer of hearts. You'd best have bought a wig, Philip."

In spite of himself, Philip laughed.

"Sir, you are incorrigible!"

"*Faute de mieux.* And whence, if I may ask, did you glean all this—sordid information, oh, my righteous son?"

"From Tom, of course. He could talk of nothing else."

"Alack! The saint is still upon his pedestal. In fact, the story was forced upon you. Philip, you enrage me." He looked up and met his son's amused glance. "Yes, child, I am enraged. Pass the wine."

Philip pushed the decanter towards him. His rather stern eyes were twinkling.

"I'll swear no one ever before possessed so outrageous a sire," he said. "I've heard of some who disinherited their sons for disreputable behaviour, but it seems you are like to disinherit me for irreproachable conduct."

"It's a *piquante* situation," agreed Sir Maurice. "But I shan't disinherit you."

"No?"

"Where's the use? With no money you could not hope to—ah—follow in my footsteps. I've a mind to turn you out of the house, though."

"Half a mind," corrected Philip. "The other half, sir, rejoices in my unblemished reputation."

"Does it?" Sir Maurice was mildly interested. "Faith, I did not know that."

"Sir, were I to break away and become as flighty as you wish, no one would be more aghast than yourself."

"You infer, my son, that I desire you to follow not in my footsteps, but in—let us say, Bancroft's. Nothing could more thoroughly disgust me."

"Ah!" Philip leant forward eagerly. "You admit that?"

Sir Maurice sipped his wine.

"Certainly. I abhor clumsiness in an *affaire*." He watched Philip draw back. "An *affaire* of the heart should be daintily conducted. A Jettan should bear in mind that for him there can be only one love; the others," he waved his hand, "should be treated with the delicacy that they deserve. Above all, they should end lightly. I would have no woman the worse for you, child, but I would have you know women and the world. I would have you experience the pleasures and the displeasures of Polite Society; I would have you taste the joys of Hazard, and the exhilaration of your sword against another's; I would have you take pains in the selection of a cravat, or the designing of a vest;

24

I would have you learn the way to turn a neat compliment and a pretty phrase; above all, I would have you know yourself, your fellow-men, and the world." He paused, studying his son. Then he smiled. "Well? What have you to say to my peroration?"

Philip answered simply, and in admiration.

"Why, sir, that I am spellbound by your fluency. In truth, Father, you have a remarkably beautiful voice."

"Bah!" snapped Sir Maurice.

CHAPTER III

Mr. Bancroft Brings Trouble into Little Fittledean

On a particularly sunny morning, some five or six days after Mr. Jettan's return from London town, the main street of Little Fittledean was made brighter still by the passage of an Apparition.

The Apparition wore a coat of palest apricot cloth, with a flowered vest of fine brocade, and startling white small-clothes. Red-heeled shoes were on his feet, and his stockings were adorned by sprawling golden clocks. He carried an amber-clouded cane and a jewelled snuff-box, while ever and anon he raised a cobwebby handkerchief to his aristocratic nose. He minced down the street towards the market-place, followed by the awestricken glances of an amazed population. The inhabitants of the village had never seen anything so wonderful or so remarkable as this gorgeous gentleman. They watched the high red heels click along the road, and admired the beautiful set of the Apparition's coat. A group of children stopped playing to stare, open-mouthed. The Apparition heeded them not. It may have been that he was oblivious of their existence. Not even when a piping treble, requested "John" to "look'ee now at them shoes!" did he show that he realised the presence of anyone but himself in the village. He minced on, very languid, and suitably bored.

Further down the street a gentleman had reined in his horse to speak to a curtseying dame, who plucked shyly at her apron, smiling up at him. Presently he, too, became aware of the sound of clicking heels. Even as the buxom dame gazed past him with wide eyes, he looked up and saw the Apparition.

I would not have you think that the Apparition noticed him. On he went, swinging his cane and yawning.

Sir Maurice turned in his saddle the better to see those pearly small-clothes. His horse cocked both ears inquiringly and blew down his nostrils.

"Well, I'm damned!" said Sir Maurice beneath his breath. "Puppy!"

Mr. Bancroft proceeded leisurely towards the market-place. He was very, very bored, and he had walked over from Great Fittledean in search of possible amusement. He almost despaired of finding it, but Fate favoured him.

Crossing the market-place, a basket on her arm and a very becoming hat tied over her curls, was Mistress Cleone. She was tripping along quite unconcernedly, her cheeks just tinged with colour, and her big eyes bluer than ever. Mr. Bancroft lost a little of his languor. It might almost be said that his eye brightened.

Cleone was coming towards him, and it was markedly evident that Mr. Bancroft made no attempt to step aside. On the contrary, he appeared to be engrossed in the contemplation of a cat right away on his left. Cleone was peeping inside her basket; she did not perceive Mr. Bancroft until she had walked into him. Then she gave a startled cry, fell back, and stared.

Mr. Bancroft was profuse in his apologies. He

swept off his hat and made her a low bow, sinking back and back on his bent left leg.

"Oh!" gasped Cleone, becomingly fluttered. "Gracious! Is it you, Mr. Bancroft?"

Mr. Bancroft said that it was. He was very modest about it, and he dubbed himself a clod-hopping oaf so to have discommoded Cleone.

Cleone dimpled, curtseyed, and prepared to go on her way. This, however, Mr. Bancroft would not allow. He insisted on taking her basket, which, he protested, was monstrous heavy for her fair hands to support.

Cleone looked up at him provocatively.

"Sir, I fear I am a stranger to you!"

"A stranger! Why, madam, is it likely that once I had seen I could ever forget your sweet face?" cried Mr. Bancroft. "Those blue eyes, madam, left a deep imprint on my soul; those soft lips—"

"But," interrupted Cleone, blushing, "my name escaped your memory. Confess, Mr. Bancroft, it is indeed so?"

Mr. Bancroft waved his handkerchief with a superb gesture.

"A name—bah! What is it? 'Tis the face that remains with me. Names do, indeed, escape me. How could a mere name conjure up this fair image?" He bowed slightly. "Your name should be Venus, madam."

"Sir!" Cleone was shocked. "I am Cleone Charteris, Mr. Bancroft," she said primly.

Mr. Bancroft was quite equal to the occasion.

"My dear," he said fondly, "do you think I did not know it?"

Cleone shook her head.

"You did not know it. And, indeed, I am prodigiously hurt and offended that you should have forgot me."

"Forgot you?" Mr. Bancroft was derisive. "Forget the little nymph who so tormented me in my youth? Fie on you, madam!"

"Oh, I did not! How can you say so, sir? 'Twas you who were always so provoking! Do you remember how we played? You and Jennifer and I and Philip— oh, and James."

"The games I remember," he answered. "But Jennifer, no. And who are Philip and James?"

"You've a monstrous short memory," reproved Cleone. "Of course you remember Philip Jettan?"

"How could I hope to remember anyone but your fair self?" he protested. "Could I be sensible of another's presence when you were there?"

Cleone giggled. She found Mr. Bancroft's compliments very entertaining and novel.

"You are quite ridiculous, sir. And this is my home."

"Alas!" sighed Mr. Bancroft. "I would it were a mile away." He opened the gate and held it for her, bowing. "May I pay my respects to Madam Charteris?" he begged.

"If you please, sir," said Cleone, eyes cast down.

They found madam in the hall, speaking to one of the servants. When she saw the resplendent Mr. Bancroft she gasped, and fell back a pace.

Bancroft stepped forward, hat in hand.

"I dare not hope for recognition, madam," he bowed. "Henry Bancroft begs you will allow him to kiss your hand."

Madam Charteris extended it weakly.

"Henry Bancroft? Gracious heaven, is it indeed you?"

Bancroft kissed the tips of her fingers, holding them lightly to his mouth with two fingers and a thumb.

"I met Mistress Cleone in the market-place," he told her. "Conceive my surprise, madam, my joyful ecstasy!"

"Indeed!" stammered madam. "In the market-place —to be sure."

"Mr. Bancroft was so kind as to relieve me of my basket," explained her daughter. "He pretends that he had not forgot me, mamma! But he cannot deceive me."

"He never sought to deceive you, Mistress Cleone. He spoke sooth when he said your image had remained with him throughout."

"Take him into the garden, Cleone," begged madam. "He will wish to see your papa."

It had not occurred to Mr. Bancroft, but he swallowed it with a good grace.

"Will you conduct me thither, Mistress Cleone?" He bowed, one arm extended.

Cleone laid the tips of her fingers on the arm.

"Certainly, sir. We shall find papa among the roses." They walked to the door.

"The roses!" sighed Mr. Bancroft. "A fit setting for your beauty, dear Cleone."

Cleone gave a little gurgle of laughter.

"'Tis papa's beauty they frame, sir, not mine," she replied.

Twenty minutes later Sir Maurice walked into the rose-garden to find Bancroft and Cleone seated in an arbour engaged in close converse, while Mr. Charteris nipped off the dead flowers near-by.

Mr. Charteris welcomed his visitor with a wave of his large scissors.

"Good day, Sir Maurice! What a very pleasant,

warm day it is, to be sure! Did you ride over to see us?"

Sir Maurice drew him apart.

"I met that—that rainbow in the village. What a plague is it? What does he do here?"

Mr. Charteris' chubby countenance was wreathed in a great, sly smile, suspiciously like a grin.

"Have you ever seen aught to equal it?" he chuckled. " 'Tis young Bancroft—in seclusion."

"I guessed as much. In seclusion, is he? Puppy!"

Mr. Charteris held up his hands.

"Oh, but Sir Maurice! A mighty soft-spoken youth —a polished gentleman, I assure you."

"Polished coxcomb!" snapped Sir Maurice. "Confound his impudence!" He turned and walked towards the arbour.

Cleone rose and came forward.

"Why, Sir Maurice! I did not see you!"

Sir Maurice raised both her hands to his lips.

"You were otherwise engaged, my dear. Will you present your cavalier?"

Cleone frowned upon him.

"Sir Maurice—! This is Mr. Bancroft, sir. Mr. Bancroft, Sir Maurice Jettan."

Mr. Bancroft's hat swept the ground. His powdered head was bent.

"I am delighted to renew my acquaintance with you, sir."

Sir Maurice inclined his head.

"I hear you intend to honour Fittledean for some few weeks?" he said. An inward laugh seemed to shake him. "You must meet my son, Philip."

"Nothing could give me more pleasure," Bancroft assured him. "I shall hope to do so at once. I am transported to meet such old friends, and to find that one"—he bowed to Cleone—"had not forgot me."

"H'm!" said Sir Maurice cryptically. Suddenly he smiled upon the younger man. "I have ridden over to beg Mr. Charteris to honour me at dinner on Wednesday—"

"Delighted, delighted!" nodded Charteris, who had joined them.

"—with madam and Cleone. You'll come, my dear? I have already spoken to your mamma."

Cleone slipped her hand in his arm.

"Why, it's very kind of you, Sir Maurice. Thank you very much."

He patted the little hand. Then he again transferred his attention to Mr. Bancroft.

"I trust you too will honour us, sir?"

"It is prodigious amiable of you, sir. I hasten to accept. On Wednesday, I think you said? With all the pleasure on earth!"

"Cleone, my dear, give me your arm as far as that rose-bush. You shall choose me a button-hole, if you will. No, no, Charteris, with her own fair fingers!" He bore Cleone away to the other end of the garden, leaving Mr. Bancroft disconsolate. When they were out of hearing Sir Maurice looked down into the roguish blue eyes. "My dear, you are a minx."

Cleone dimpled charmingly.

"I don't know why you should say so, sir."

"Of course not," agreed Sir Maurice. "Now what is the game? It's to make Philip jealous, eh?"

"Sir! How can you?"

"My love, I know all about you, for I am an old man. Make Philip jealous by all means."

"I'm sure I never—"

"Of course not. But I think, with you, that it would be a very good plan. The boy is too stolid and cock-sure."

"Cock— Oh, indeed!"

"So if you shake Philip up from his toes to his head —you'll earn a father's blessing."

Cleone controlled a trembling lip.

"Sir—you are—a very naughty—conspirator."

"We'll leave it at that," said Sir Maurice. "Now choose me a rose, little witch. Gad, if I were ten years younger I'd make Philip jealous myself!"

Cleone tip-toed, her hands on his shoulders.

"You are very, very wicked," she told him gravely.

Sir Maurice kissed her.

"So are you, minx, and I want you for my daughter. We are so well suited."

Cleone blushed fiery red and hid her face in his coat.

Sir Maurice rode home wrapped in thought. Now and again he chuckled softly to himself, but when later he met his son he was as solemn as ever.

Philip came into the library, riding-whip in hand. He had been on the fields all the morning, and Sir Maurice eyed his boots with disfavour. Philip sank into a chair.

"Two of the big meadows are cut, sir. We should finish by next week." He glanced anxiously out of the window. "I hope the rain holds off."

"Oh, it will," replied his father placidly.

"I am not so sure. Last summer the hay was black. Did you—er—did you ride into the village?"

"I did."

"And—and did you go to—Sharley House?"

"Ay."

"Are they—did they accept?" Philip played with his whip, feigning unconcern.

"They did. I met that fellow Bancroft."

"Oh!" said Philip. "Where?"

"In the rose-garden," yawned Sir Maurice.

The whip fell to the ground.

"What? In the rose-garden? Whose rose-garden?"

"At Sharley House, of course."

"Where—was— What was he doing there?"

"He was sitting in the arbour, talking to Cleone."

"Confound him!" growled Philip, as if his worst fears were realised. "What's he like?"

Sir Maurice glanced across at him.

"He is about your height—perhaps a little taller. He —ah—seems to have a soft tongue and an engaging manner."

"Oh, has he?" Philip's voice was startlingly grim.

"He and Cleone were renewing their old friendship."

"Oh, were they? What old friendship? He was never our friend!"

"No, I suppose not," said Sir Maurice innocently. "He is some six or seven years older than you, is he not?"

"Five!" said Philip emphatically.

"Only five? Of course, he looks and seems older, but he has seen more of the world, which accounts for it."

To this Philip vouchsafed no answer at all, but he looked at his father with some suspicion. Sir Maurice allowed two or three minutes to elapse before he spoke again.

"By the way, Philip, Bancroft dines with us on Wednesday."

Up sprang Philip in great annoyance.

"What's that, sir? Dines here, and on Wednesday? Surely you did not invite the fellow?"

"But I did," answered Sir Maurice blandly. "Why not?"

"Why not? What do we want with him?"

"It remains to be seen." Sir Maurice hid a smile. "Bancroft is most desirious of meeting you."

Philip made a sound betwixt a grunt and a snort.

"More like he wishes to pursue his acquaintance with Cl—Mistress Cleone," he retorted.

"Well, she's a pretty piece," said his father.

Philip glared at him.

"If I find him annoying Cleone with his damned officious attentions, I'll—I'll—"

"Oh, I do not think she is annoyed," replied Sir Maurice.

At that Philip stalked out of the room, leaving his father a prey to indecent mirth.

CHAPTER IV

The Trouble Comes to a Head

At half-past five on Wednesday Mr. Henry Bancroft was ushered into the withdrawing-room at the Pride. He was, as he had intended he should be, the last to arrive.

Sir Maurice stood in front of the empty grate, talking to Mr. Charteris; madam sat on a couch, her daughter beside her, and Philip near-by. They all looked up as Mr. Bancroft was announced, and Philip rose, for the first time in his life acutely conscious of an ill-fitting coat and unpowdered hair.

Mr. Bancroft was a dream of lilac and rose. He might have been dressed for a ball, thought Cleone. Diamonds and rubies flashed from his buckles, and from his cravat; a diamond clasp was above the riband that tied his wig. He minced forward daintily and bowed, one be-ringed hand over his heart.

Sir Maurice came forward, very stately in black with touches of purple.

"Ah, Mr. Bancroft! I need not present you to the ladies, I know." He paused to allow Bancroft to throw a languishing glance towards the couch. "I think you and my son are not altogether unknown to one another?"

Bancroft turned on his heel to face Philip. He bowed again, slightly flourishing his handkerchief.

"My playmate of long ago," he murmured. "Your very obedient, Mr. Jettan."

Philip returned the bow awkwardly.

"I am very pleased to meet you again, sir," he said, determined to be polite to this most obnoxious guest. "Do you—er—intend to make a long stay?"

Bancroft raised his shoulders and spread out his hands.

"I had thought not, sir, but now"—another glance was cast at Cleone—"I think—perhaps—!" he smiled, running quick, appraising eyes over Philip's person. "Do you know, sir, I swear I'd not have known you. You have grown prodigiously."

Cleone broke into the conversation.

"You were so much older than Philip, or James or me, Mr. Bancroft!"

Instantly he swept round.

"I thank you for the past tense, Mistress Cleone! At least, I am no longer so aged."

"Why, sir, have you lost your years?" she asked.

"In your company, yes, madam. Can you wonder?"

"Oh, I am monstrous flattered, sir!" Cleone spread out her fan and held it before her face.

"Not flattered, Mistress Cleone; justly appreciated."

"La!" said Madam Charteris. "How can you say such things, Mr. Bancroft? I declare you will make my daughter vain!"

"Vanity, madam, mates not with such beauty as that of your daughter," he retaliated. To the right he could see Philip, glowering, and his mischievous soul laughed. Then Sir Maurice claimed his attention, and he turned away.

Philip walked to the couch and stood behind it, resting his arm on the back. He leaned over Cleone with an air of possession.

"Pranked out mummer!" he muttered in her ear.

Cleone smiled up at him.

"Why, sir, are you at variance with him in the matter of my looks?" she asked, and thereby bereft him of speech. Her smile turned to a look of reproach. " 'Tis your cue, sir; am I to be slighted?"

A dull red crept to the roots of Philip's hair. He spoke lower still.

"You know—what I think of you, Cleone. I cannot —mouth what I feel—in pretty phrases."

A strangely tender light came into her eyes.

"You might try, Philip," she said.

"What, here? Not I! I am not one to sing your charms in public." He laughed shortly. "So that is what you desire?"

The tender light died.

"No, sir. I desire you will not lean so close. You inconvenience me."

Philip straightened at once, but he still stood behind her. Bancroft met his eyes and was quick to read the challenge they held. He smiled, twirling his eyeglass.

When dinner was announced, Cleone was talking to Bancroft. It was but natural that he should offer her his arm, but to Philip it seemed a most officious, impudent action. Sir Maurice led Madam Charteris into the dining-room; Mr. Charteris and Philip brought up the rear.

From Philip's point of view the meal was not a success. Seated side by side, Cleone and Bancroft exchanged a flood of conversation. Philip, at the foot of the table, had on his right Mr. Bancroft, and on his left Mr. Charteris. To the latter he made grave conversation. Occasionally Bancroft dragged him into a discussion; once or twice Madam Charteris and Sir

Maurice appealed to him. But Cleone seemed unaware of his existence. She was very gay, too; her eyes sparkled and shone, her cheeks were faintly flushed. She answered Mr. Bancroft's sallies with delightful little laughs and applause.

As the dinner proceeded, Philip was made to feel more than ever his own shortcomings. When he looked at Mr. Bancroft's white hands with their highly polished nails, and many rings, he compared them with his strong brown ones, tanned and—coarse? Covertly he inspected them; no, they were better hands than that nincompoop's, but his nails . . . bah! only fops such as this puppy polished their nails! . . .

The lilac satin of Mr. Bancroft's coat shimmered in the light of the candles. How tightly it fitted him across the shoulders! How heavily it was laced, and how full were its skirts! A coat for a drawing-room! Unconsciously Philip squared his shoulders. All that foaming lace . . . more suited to a woman than to a man. The quizzing-glass . . . abominable affectation! The jewels . . . flaunting them in the country! Patched and painted, mincing, prattling puppy-dog! How could Cleone bear him so near, with his fat, soft hands, and his person reeking of some sickly scent? . . .

Now he was talking of town and its allure, toying with the names of first one celebrity and then another. And Cleone drinking in the silly, smug talk! . . . Now hints at conquests made—veiled allusions to his own charms. Ape!—truckling, overdressed ape! Suddenly Philip wanted to throw his glass at Bancroft. He choked down the mad impulse, and strove to listen to Mr. Charteris.

Back in the withdrawing-room again it was worse. Sir Maurice asked Cleone to sing, and she went to the spinet. Bancroft followed, to choose her music, to turn the pages, to gaze at her in frank admiration. Damn him, damn him, damn him!

The party came to an end at last; Philip was alone with his father. Sir Maurice leaned his chin in his hand, watching him amusedly. For a long while Philip said nothing, but presently he brought his eyes away from the window and looked at his father.

"And that," he said bitingly, "is what you would have me. A conceited, painted puppy, fawning and leering on every woman that crosses his path!"

"Not at all." Sir Maurice took out his snuff-box and opened it. "'Tis the last thing in the world I would have you."

"You said—"

"I said I would have you a very perfect gentleman, knowing the world and its ways."

"Well?—"

"You perhaps conceive Mr. Bancroft a perfect gentleman?"

"Not I! 'Tis you who—"

Sir Maurice raised one delicate hand.

"Pardon me! You choose to assume that I thought it. Mr. Bancroft is, as you so truly remark, a conceited, painted puppet. But he apes, so far as he is able, the thing that I am; that I wish you to become. You are a country-bumpkin, my dear; he is a coddled doll. Strive to become something betwixt the two."

"I had sooner be what I am!"

"Which is a conceited oaf."

"Sir!"

Sir Maurice rose, leaning on his cane.

"Remain what you are, my son, but bethink you—which will Cleone prefer? Him who gives her graceful homage, and charms her ears with honeyed words, or him who is tongue-tied before her, who is careless of his appearance, and who treats her, not as a young and beautiful girl, but as his inevitable possession?"

Philip answered quickly.

"Cleone, sir, will—give herself where she pleases, but she is not one to over-rate the tricks of such as Bancroft."

"Or to under-rate the discomforts of tying herself to one who is tied to the soil and his own pleasure," said Sir Maurice softly.

The grey eyes met his, a trifle hurt.

"I am selfish, Father? Because I will not become the thing I despise?"

"And narrow, Philip, to despise what you do not know."

"Thank you!" The young voice was exceedingly bitter. "I am to be a painted popinjay! I tell you, sir, Cleone must take me as I am."

"Or leave you as you are," said Sir Maurice gently.

"A warning, sir?"

"That's for you to judge, child. And now I'll to bed." He paused, looking at his son.

Philip went to him.

"Good-night, sir."

Sir Maurice smiled, holding out his hand.

"Good-night, my son."

Philip kissed his fingers.

Followed a week of disturbing trivialities. Mr. Bancroft was more often in Little Fittledean than at home, and most often at Sharley House. He there met Philip, not once, but many times, hostile and possessive. He laughed softly, and sought to engage Philip in a war of wits, but Philip's tongue was stiff and reluctant. So Mr. Bancroft made covert sport of him and renewed his attentions to Cleone.

Cleone herself was living in a strange whirl. There was much in Mr. Bancroft that displeased her; I do not think she ever had it in her mind to wed him, which was perhaps fortunate, as Mr. Bancroft certainly had it not in his. But homage is grateful to women, and ardent yet dainty love-making fascinating to the young. She played with Mr. Bancroft, but thought no less of Philip. Yet Philip contrived to irritate her. His air of ownership, his angry, reproachful looks, fired the spirit of coquetry within her. Mastery thrilled her, but a mastery that offered to take all, giving nothing, annoyed her. That Philip loved her to distraction, she knew; also she knew that Philip would expect her to bend before his will. He would not change, it would be she who must conform to his pleasure. Philip was determined to remain as he was, faithful but dull. She wanted all that he despised: life, gaiety, society, and frivolity. She weighed the question carefully, a little too carefully for a maid in love. She wanted Philip and she did not want him. As he was, she would have none of him; as she wished him to be, he might have her. But for the present she was no man's, and no man had the right to chide her. Philip had made a mistake in his wooing in showing her how much his own he thought her. All unwitting, he was paving the way to his own downfall.

Despite the lisping conceit of Mr. Bancroft, his polished phrases and his elegancy when compared with Philip's brusqueness threw Philip in the shade. Mr. Bancroft could taunt and gibe at Philip, sure of triumph; Philip tied his tongue in knots and relapsed into silence, leaving Mr. Bancroft to shine in his victory.

43

The man Cleone chose to wed must be a match for all, with words or swords. Cleone continued to smile upon Mr. Bancroft.

At the end of the week the trouble came to a head. In the garden of Sharley House, before Cleone, Mr. Bancroft threw veiled taunts at Philip, and very thinly veiled sneers. He continued to hold the younger man's lack of polish up to scorn, always smiling and urbane.

Cleone recognised the gleam in Philip's eye. She was a little frightened and sought to smooth over the breach. But when she presently retired to the house, Philip arrested Mr. Bancroft, who was following.

"A word with you, sir."

Bancroft turned, brows raised, lips curled almost sneeringly.

Philip stood very straight, shoulders squared.

"You have seen fit to mock at me, sir—"

"I—" interpolated Bancroft languidly. "My dear sir!"

"—and I resent it. There is that in your manner to which I object."

Bancroft's brows rose higher.

"To—which—you—object . . ." he echoed softly.

"I trust I make myself clear?" snapped Philip.

Bancroft raised his eyeglass. Through it he studied Philip from his toes to his head.

"Is it possible that you want satisfaction?" he drawled.

"More than that," retorted Philip. "It is certain."

Once again he was scrutinised. Mr. Bancroft's smile grew.

"I do not fight with schoolboys," he said.

The colour flooded Philip's face.

"Perhaps because you are afraid," he said quickly, guarding his temper.

44

"Perhaps," nodded Bancroft. "Yet I have not the reputation of a coward."

Swift as a hawk Philip pounced.

"You have, sir, as I well know, the reputation of a libertine!"

It was Bancroft's turn to flush.

"I—beg—your—pardon?"

"It is necessary," bowed Philip, enjoying himself now for the first time in many days.

"You—impudent boy!" gasped Bancroft.

"I would sooner be that, sir, than an impudent, painted puppy."

Under his powder Bancroft was fiery red.

"I see you will have it, Mr. Jettan. I will meet you when and where you will."

Philip patted his sword-hilt, and Bancroft observed for the first time that he was wearing a sword.

"I have noticed, Mr. Bancroft, that you habitually don your sword. So I took the precaution of wearing mine. 'When' is now, and 'where' is yonder!" He pointed above the hedge that encircled the garden to the copse beyond. It was a very fine theatrical effect, and he was pleased with it.

Bancroft sneered at him.

"A trifle countrified, Mr. Jettan. Do you propose to dispense with such needless formalities as seconds?"

"I think we can trust each other," said Philip grandly.

"Then pray lead the way," bowed Bancroft.

What followed was not so fine. Bancroft was proficient in the art of the duello; Philip had never fought in his life. Fencing had never interested him, and Sir Maurice had long since despaired of teaching him anything more than the rudiments. However, he was very angry and very reckless, while Bancroft thought

45

to play with him. He thrust so wildly and so insanely that Bancroft was taken unawares and received a fine slash across the arm. After that he fenced more carefully, and in a very short time pinked Philip neatly and artistically above the elbow of his sword arm. As Philip's blade wavered and fell, he wiped his own on his handkerchief, sheathed it, and bowed.

"Let this be a lesson to you, sir," he said, and walked away before Philip could pick up his sword.

Twenty minutes later Philip walked into the hall of Sharley House, a handkerchief tied tightly round his arm, and asked for Mistress Cleone. On being told that she was in the parlour, he stalked in upon her.

Cleone's eyes flew to his crooked arm.

"Oh!" she cried, and half rose. "What—what have you done? You are hurt!"

"It is less than nothing, I thank you," replied Philip. "I want you to answer me plainly, Cleone. What is that fellow to you?"

Cleone sat down again. Her eyes flashed; Philip was nearer than ever to his downfall.

"I entirely fail to understand you, sir," she answered.

"Do you love that—that prancing ninny?" asked Philip.

"I consider such a question an—an impertinence!" cried Cleone. "What right have you to ask me such a thing?"

Philip's brows met across the bridge of his nose.

"You do love him?"

"No, I don't I mean— Oh, how dare you?"

Philip came closer. The frown faded.

"Cleone—do you—could you—love me?"

Cleone was silent.

Closer still came Philip, and spoke rather huskily.

46

"Will you—marry me, Cleone?"

Still silence, but the blue eyes were downcast.

"Cleone," blundered Philip, "you—don't want a—mincing, powdered—beau."

"I do not want a—a—raw—country-bumpkin," she said cruelly.

Philip drew himself up.

"That is what you think me, Cleone?"

Something in his voice brought tears to her eyes.

"I—no—I—oh, Philip, I *could* not marry you as you are!"

"No?" Philip spoke very evenly. "But if I became—your ideal—you could marry me?"

"I—oh, you should not—ask such questions!"

"As I am—you'll none of me. You do not want—an honest man's love. You want the pretty compliments of a doll. If I will learn to be—a doll—you'll wed me. Well, I will learn. You shall not be—annoyed—by an honest man's love—any longer. I will go to London—and one day I'll return. Farewell, Cleone."

"Oh—goodness—are you—going to town?" she gasped.

"Since that is your desire, yes," he answered.

She held out her hand, and when he kissed it her fingers clung for an instant.

"Come back to me, Philip," she whispered.

He bowed, still holding her hand, and then, without a word, released it, and marched out, very dignified. It was another fine tragic effect, but Cleone, when the door closed behind him, broke into an hysterical laugh. She was rather amazed, and a little apprehensive.

CHAPTER V

In which Philip Finds that his Uncle is More Sympathetic than his Father

Home went Philip, a prey to conflicting emotions. He was angry with Cleone, and hurt at what he termed her fickleness, but she was very lovely, and still wholly desirable. Never until now had he realized how necessary she was to his happiness. She would not marry him unless he reformed, learned to behave like Bancroft—that was what she meant. She did not love him as he was; she wanted polish, and frills and furbelows. Philip's lips tightened. She should have them—but he was very, very angry. Then he thought of his father, and the anger grew. What right had these two to seek to change him into something that was utterly insincere, trifling, and unmanly? His father would be rejoiced to hear that he was going 'to become a gentleman'. Even he had no use for Philip as he was. Well, they should have what they wanted —and then perhaps they would be sorry. In a wave of self-pity he considered how dearly he loved these two people. He wanted neither to change, he loved them for what they were; but they . . . He felt very sore and ill-used. Something else there was that troubled him. He had set about the task of punishing Mr. Bancroft, and Mr. Bancroft had ended by punishing him. No pleasant thought, that. Bancroft was master not only of words but of swords; he, Philip, was master of

49

neither. He brooded over the question, chafed and irritable. And so came home to Sir Maurice.

He found him seated on the terrace, reading Juvenal. Sir Maurice, glancing up, observed Philip's sling. He said nothing, but his eyes gleamed an instant.

Philip threw himself down upon a bench.

"Well, sir, Bancroft and I have met."

"I thought it would come," nodded his father.

"I'm no match for him. He—pinked me with some ease."

Again Sir Maurice nodded.

"Also"—Philip spoke with difficulty—"Cleone—will have none of me—as I am." He looked across at his father with some bitterness. "As you prophesied, sir, she prefers the attentions of such as Bancroft."

"And so—?"

Philip was silent.

"And so Mr. Jettan withdraws from the lists. Very fine," added Sir Maurice.

"Have I said so, sir?" Philip spoke sharply. "Cleone desires a beau—she shall have one! I have told her that I shall not come to her until I am what—she thinks—is her desire! I will show her and you that I am not the dull-witted bumpkin you think me, fit for nothing better than"—he mimicked his father's tone—"to till the earth! I'll learn to be the painted fop you'd like to see me! Neither you nor she shall be offended longer by the sight of me as I am!"

"Now, here's a heat!" remarked Sir Maurice. "So you'll to London, boy? To your uncle?"

Philip shrugged.

"As well to him as any other. I care not."

"That's the wrong spirit for your emprise," said Sir Maurice, a laugh in his eyes. "You must enter into your venture heart and soul."

Philip flung out his arm.

"My heart's here, sir, at home!"

"It's also at Sharley House," said his father dryly, "or why do you go to London?"

"Ay, it's there! And I have the felicity of knowing that Cleone cares not one snap of her fingers for me! She trifles with me, and makes a sport of me for her amusement!"

"Tra-la-la-la!" said Sir Maurice. "Then why go to London?"

"To show her that I am not the brainless oaf she thinks me!" answered Philip, and marched off.

Sir Maurice returned to Juvenal.

Not until his arm was healed did Philip set forth to London town. He parted amicably enough from his father, who gave him much advice, many introductions, and his blessing. Cleone he did not see at all, but when he had gone she went up to the Pride and held Sir Maurice's hand very tightly. She shed a few tears; also she laughed a little. As for Sir Maurice—well, he chid himself for a sentimental old fool, but with Philip's departure had come a void which could only be filled by Philip's return.

Tom was breakfasting when his nephew was announced. It was noon, but Tom had spent a strenuous night. Philip walked into the room, under the gloomy eye of Moggat, travel-stained and stiff from the saddle. He was quite unexpected, but his uncle showed no surprise at seeing him.

"Well met, Philip, my boy! What's to do now?"

Philip sank into a chair.

"I'll tell you when I'm fed," he grinned. "That sirloin pleases my eye."

"Not an artistic colour," said Tom, studying it, "but appetising, I grant you."

"Artistic be damned!" said Philip, attacking it. Then he frowned. "H'm! No, Tom, 'tis a displeasing blend —red and brown."

Tom looked at him in surprise.

"What's colour to you, Philip?"

"Naught, God help me," answered Philip, and fell to with a will.

"I echo that sentiment," said Tom. "How does your father?"

"Well enough; he sends you his love."

Tom thereupon buried himself in the mass of correspondence that lay by his plate. When he came to the end, Philip had finished his repast. Tom pushed back his chair.

"Well, Philip, what brings you here? Moggat, you rascal, away with you!"

Philip waited until the door had closed upon Moggat's reluctant back.

"I've—to learn to be—a gentleman," he said.

Tom stared at him. Then he burst out laughing.

"God ha' mercy, Philip, has it come to that?"

"I do not take your meaning," said Philip crossly.

"What! It's not a petticoat?"

"Tom, I'll thank you to—to—be quiet!"

Tom choked his laughter.

"Oh, I'm dumb! How do you propose to set about the task?"

" 'Tis what I want to know, Tom."

"And I'm to teach you?"

Philip hesitated.

"Is it perhaps—a thing I can best learn alone?" he asked, surprisingly diffident.

"What is it exactly you want to learn?"

"To become a gentleman. Have I not said it?"

"Odd rot, what are ye now?"

Philip's lips curled.

"I have it on the best authority, Tom, that I am a clumsy, witless clod-hopper."

His uncle regarded him with some kindliness.

"Little vixen," he remarked sapiently.

"I beg your pardon?" Philip was cold.

"Not at all," said Tom hastily. "So Maurice has been at you again, eh? Now, Philip, lad, come off your pinnacle and be sensible, for God's sake! What do ye want?"

"I want, or rather, they—he—wants me to learn how to dress, how to walk across a room, how to play with words, how to make love to women, how to bow, how to—"

"Oh, stop, stop!" cried Tom. "I have the whole picture! And it's no easy task, my boy. It will take you years to learn."

"Why, I trust you're pessimistic, sir," said Philip, "for I intend to acquire all these arts—within a year."

"Well, I like your spirit," acknowledged Tom. "Take some more ale, lad, and let me have the whole story."

This advice Philip saw fit to follow. In a very short time he found that he had unburdened his sore heart to an astonishingly sympathetic uncle. Tom forbore to laugh—although now and then he was seized by an inward paroxysm which he had much ado to choke down. When Philip came to the end of his recital and stared gloomily across at him, he tapped his teeth with one polished finger-nail and looked exceeding wise.

"My opinion is, Philip, that you are the best of all us Jettans, but that's neither here nor there. Now it

53

seems to me that the folk at home don't appreciate your sterling qualities—"

"Oh, 'tis not my qualities they object to! 'Tis my lack of vice."

"Don't interrupt my peroration, lad. They think you a noble—what was the word you used?—clod-hopper. 'Tis marvellously apt. They doubt your ability to shine in society. 'Tis for us to prove them to be mistaken. You must surprise them."

"I doubt I shall," said Philip, with the glimmering of a smile.

Tom was wrapped in thought; his eyes ran over his nephew's form appraisingly.

"Ye've a fine figure, and good legs. Your hands?"

Philip extended them, laughing.

"Um! a little attention, and I'd not wish to see better. Like all the Jettans, you are passable of countenance, not to say handsome."

"Am I?" Philip was startled. "I never knew that before!"

"Then ye know it now. You're the spit of your father in his young days. Gad, what days they were! Before I grew fat," he added sadly. "But I wander, I wander. Maurice and the petticoat—what's the girl's name?"

"I don't see why you should assu—"

"Don't be a fool, lad! It's that fair chit, eh? Charlotte—no, damn it, some heathenish name!"

"Cleone," supplied Philip, submitting.

"Ay, that's it—Cleone. Well, Maurice and Cleone think that ye'll gain a little polish and some style. What you must do is to excel. Excel!"

"I doubt I could not," said Philip. "And, indeed, I've no mind to."

"Then I've done with you." Tom leaned back in his chair with an air of finality.

"No, no, Tom! You must help me!"

A stern eye was fixed on him.

"Ye must put yourself in my hands, then."

"Ay, but—"

"Completely," said Tom inexorably.

Philip collapsed.

"Oh, very well!"

The round, good-tempered face lost its unaccustomed severity. Tom was again wrapped in thought.

"Paris," he said at length, to the bewilderment of his nephew. "You must go there," he explained.

Philip was horrified.

"What! I? To Paris? Never!"

"Then I wash my—"

"But, Tom, consider! I know so little French!"

"The more reason."

"But—but—damn it, I say I will not!"

Tom yawned.

"As ye will."

Philip became more and more unhappy.

"Why should I go to Paris?" he growled.

"You're like a surly bear," reproved Tom. "Where else would you go?"

"Can't I—surely I can learn all I want here?"

"Ay, and have all your friends nudging each other as you transform from what you are to what you are to become!"

Philip had not thought of that. He relapsed into sulky silence.

"To Paris," resumed Tom, "within the week. Luckily, you've more money than is good for you. You've no need to pinch and scrape. I'll take you, clothe you, and introduce you."

Philip brightened.

"Will you? That's devilish good of you, Tom!"

"It is," agreed Tom. "But I dare swear I'll find entertainment there." He chuckled. "And not a word to your father or to anyone. You'll vanish, and when you reappear no one will know you."

This dazzling prospect did not appear to allure Philip. He sighed heavily.

"I suppose I must do it. But—" He rose and walked to the window. "It's all that I despise and that I detest. Mere love—does not suffice. Well, we shall see." He thrust his hands deep in his pockets. "The thing they want me to be is neither noble nor estimable. They—he—they—don't care what may be a man's reputation or his character! He must speak them softly, and charm their ears with silly compliments, and their eyes with pretty silks and satins. Naught else is of consequence. Faugh!"

"Ay, you're taking it hard," nodded his uncle. "But they're all the same, lad—bless 'em!"

"I thought—this one—was different."

"More fool you," said Tom cynically.

CHAPTER VI

The Beginning of the Transformation

Philip stood in the middle of the floor, expostulating. A sleek valet was kneeling before him, coaxing his gold-clocked stockings over the knee of his small-clothes, and a middle-aged exquisite was arranging his Mechlin cravat for the seventh time, a frown crinkling his forehead, and French oaths proceeding from his tinted lips. Mr. Thomas Jettan was giving the nails of Philip's right hand a last, lingering polish. And Philip, supremely miserable, expostulated in vain.

François sat back on his heels and eyed Philip's legs adoringly.

"But of an excellence, m'sieur! So perfect a calf, m'sieur! So vairy fine a laig," he explained in English.

Philip tried to squint down at them, and was rewarded by an impatient exclamation from the gentleman who was wrestling with his cravat.

"*Tais-toi, imbécile!* 'Ow is it zat I shall arrange your cravat if you tweest and turn like zis? Lift your chin, Philippe!"

"*Mais, monsieur, je—je—cela me donne—mal au cou.*"

"*Il faut souffrir pour être bel,*" replied the Marquis severely.

"So it seems," said Philip irritably. "Tom, for God's sake, have done!"

His uncle chuckled.

"I've finished, never fear. Jean, that is wonderful!"

Le Marquis de Château-Banvau stepped back to view his handiwork.

"I am not altogether satisfied," he said musingly.

Philip warded him off.

"No, no, m'sieur! I am sure it is perfection!"

The Marquis disregarded him. Once more his nimble fingers busied themselves amongst the folds of soft lace. His eyes gleamed suddenly.

"It is well! François, the sapphire pin! Quickly!"

The valet held it out. He and Tom watched anxiously as the Marquis' hand hovered, uncertain. Philip felt that this was a supreme moment; he held his breath. Then the pin was fixed with one unerring movement, and the two onlookers drew deep breaths of relief.

The Marquis nodded.

"Yes, Tom, you are right. It is a triumph. Sit down, Philippe."

Philip sank into a chair by the dressing-table.

"What now? Have you nearly finished?"

"Now the rouge. François, haste!"

Philip tried to rebel.

"I will not be painted and powdered!"

The Marquis fixed him with a cold eye.

"*Plaît-il?*"

"M'sieur—I—I will not!"

"Philippe—if it were not for the love I bear your papa, I would leave you zis minute. You will do as I say, *hein?*"

"But, m'sieur, can I not go without paint?"

"You can not."

58

Philip smiled ruefully.

"Then do your worst!"

"It is not my worst, *ingrat.* It is my best!"

"Your best, then. I am really very grateful, sir."

The Marquis' lips twitched. He signed to François.

Under his deft hands Philip squirmed and screwed up his face. He complained that the haresfoot tickled him, and he winced when the Marquis pressed two patches on his face. When François dusted his cheeks with powder he sneezed, and when a single sapphire ear-ring was placed in his left ear he scowled and muttered direfully.

But the supreme torture was to come. He discovered that it required the united energies of the three men to coax him into his coat. When at last it was on he assured them it would split across the shoulders if he so much as moved a finger.

The Marquis found him *fort amusant,* but troublesome.

"Forget it, little fool!"

"Forget it?" cried Philip. "How can I forget it when it prevents my moving?"

"*Quelle absurdité!* The sword, Tom!"

"How can I dance in a sword?" protested Philip.

"It is *de rigueur,*" said the Marquis.

Philip fingered the jewelled hilt.

"A pretty plaything," he said. "I have never spent so much money on fripperies before."

François arranged the full skirts of his coat about the sword, and Tom slipped rings on to Philip's fingers. A point-edged hat was put into his hand, an enamelled snuff-box, and a handkerchief.

Thomas looked at the Marquis, the Marquis nodded complacently. He led Philip to a long glass.

"Well, my friend?"

But Philip said never a word. He stared and stared again at his reflection. He could not believe that it was himself. He saw a tall, slight figure dressed in a pale blue satin coat, and white small-clothes, flowered waistcoat, and gold-clocked stockings. High red-heeled shoes, diamond-buckled, were on his feet, lace foamed over his hands and at his neck, while a white wig, marvellously curled and powdered, replaced his shorn locks. Unconsciously he drew himself up, tilting his chin a little and shook out his handkerchief.

"Well!" The Marquis grew impatient. "You have nothing to say?"

Philip turned.

"*C'est merveilleux!*" he breathed.

The Marquis beamed, but he shook his head.

"In time, yes. At present, a thousand times no! *C'est gauche, c'est impossible!*"

Unwontedly humble, Philip begged to be made less *gauche.*

"It is my intention," said the Marquis. "A month or so and I shall be proud of my pupil."

"Faith, I'm proud of ye now!" cried Tom. "Why, lad, you'll be more modish than ever Maurice was!"

Philip flushed beneath his powder. A ruby on his finger caught his eye. He regarded it for a moment, frowning, then he took it off.

"Oh?" queried the Marquis. "Why?"

"I don't like it."

"You don't like it? Why not?"

"I don't know. I'll only wear sapphires and diamonds."

"By heaven, the boy's right!" exclaimed Tom. "He should be all blue!"

"In a month—two months—I shall present you at

Versailles," decided the Marquis. "François, remove that abominable ruby. And now—*en avant!*"

And so went Philip to his first ball.

At the end of the month Tom went home to London, having set his nephew's feet on the path he was to tread. He left him in charge of M. de Château-Banvau, who had by now developed a lively interest in him.

After that first ball Philip threw off the last shreds of rebellion; he played his part well, and he became very busy. Every morning he fenced with an expert until he had acquired some skill with a small-sword; he spoke nothing but French from morn to night; he permitted the Marquis to introduce him into society; he strove to loosen his tongue, and he paid flippant court to several damsels who ogled him for his fine appearance, until his light conversation grew less forced and uncomfortable. For a while he took no interest in his tailoring, allowing Tom or François to garb him as they pleased. But one day, when François extended a pair of cream stockings to his gaze, he eyed them through his quizzing-glass for a long moment. Then he waved them aside.

François was hurt; he liked those stockings. Would not M'sieur consider them? M'sieur most emphatically would not. If François admired pink clocks on a cream ground, let him take the stockings. M'sieur would not wear them; they offended him.

Before very long 'le jeune Anglais' was looked for and welcomed. Ladies liked him for his firm chin, and his palpable manliness; men liked him for his modesty and his money. He was invited to routs and *bals masqués,* and to card-parties and *soirées.* Philip began to enjoy himself; he was tasting the delights of popularity. Bit by bit he grew to expect invitations from these new acquaintances. But still M. le Marquis was dissatisfied. It was all very well, but not well enough for him.

However, it was quite well enough for Thomas, and he departed, chuckling and elated. He left Philip debating over two wigs and the arrangement of his jewels.

Hardly a fortnight later Philip made secure his position in Polite Society by fighting a duel with a jealous husband. Lest you should be shocked at this sudden depravity, I will tell you that there was little enough cause for fighting, as Philip considered the lady as he might consider an aunt. Happily she was unaware of this. Philip's friends did not hold back; he had no difficulty in finding seconds, and the *affaire* ended in a neat thrust which pinked the husband, and a fresh wave of popularity for Philip.

The Marquis told his pupil that he was a gay dog, and was met by a chilling stare.

"I—beg—your pardon?" said Philip stiffly.

"But what a modesty!" cried the Marquis, much amused.

"Is it conceivable that you think me attracted by the smiles of Madame de Foli-Martin?"

"But yes! Of course I think it!"

"Permit me to enlighten you," said Philip. "My affections are with a lady—at home."

"Oh, la, la!" deplored the Marquis. "A lady of the country? A simple country wench?"

"I thank God, yes," said Philip. He depressed his

friend, who had hoped for better things of him. But he thought it wiser to change the subject.

"Philip, I will take you to Court."

Philip crossed one elegantly breeched leg over the other. He was, if anything, a little bored.

"Yes? Next week, perhaps? I am very much engaged until then."

The shrewd eyes twinkled.

"The manner is excellent, my friend. You will like to make your bow to the King."

Philip shrugged.

"Certainly. I trust the King will consider himself sufficiently honoured."

"*Sans doute,*" bowed the Marquis. "But I counsel you, slayer of hearts, to cast your eyes away from la Pompadour."

"M'sieur, I have already told you—"

"Oh, yes. But you have now the name for—slaying of hearts."

Philip dropped his affectation.

"Good gad! Do you say so, sir? I?"

"It is very fashionable," said the Marquis mischievously. "You become a figure."

"But I—" He checked himself, and relapsed into languor. "They fatigue me." And he yawned.

"What! Even la Salévier?"

"The woman with the enormous wig—oh—ah! She is well enough, but *passée, mon cher Marquis, passée!*"

"*Sangdieu,* you are fastidious of a sudden! Is the little country chit so lovely?"

"Your pardon, Marquis, but I prefer to leave that lady's name out of this or any discussion."

"Or I shall have a small-sword through my heart, *hein?*"

Philip smiled.

"That is absurd, sir."

That night he gave a card-party. The play was high and the bottles numerous. He lost some money, won a little, and was put to bed by his valet long after dawn. He awoke later with a splitting headache, but he considered himself a man. That was in September.

CHAPTER VII

Mr. Bancroft Comes to Paris and is Annoyed

In February came Mr. Bancroft to Paris. Philip's departure from Little Fittledean had been closely followed by his own, for he found that Cleone no longer smiled. Also, the spice of wooing her was gone when there was no jealous lover to flout. He waited until his *affaire* had blown over, and then he went back to London. Now, very blasé, he came to Paris in search of new pastimes.

It was not long before he met Philip. And the manner of the meeting was delightfully sensational. Under the auspices of his friend, M. de Chambert, he attended a rout at the hotel of the Duchesse de Maugry. He was presented to one Mademoiselle de Chaucheron, a sprightly little lady, with roguish black eyes. Mr. Bancroft was content to form one of the small court she held. Several old acquaintances he met, for he was not unknown in Paris.

Conversation flourished for some time. But suddenly Mademoiselle cried out, clapping her hands:

"*Le voilà, notre petit Philippe! Eh bien, petit Anglais?*"

A slight gentleman in peach-coloured satin, powdered, painted, perfumed, came quickly through the group and went down on one knee before her.

"At thy most exquisite feet, my lady!"

Delighted, she gave him her hand to kiss.

"And where have you been this long while, *vaurien?*"

Philip kissed the tips of her fingers, one by one.

"Languishing in outer darkness, *chérie.*"

"The darkness of the Court!" laughed the Comte de Saint-Dantin. "Philippe, I know you for a rogue and a trifler!"

Philip looked up, still holding Mademoiselle's hand.

"Someone has maligned me. Of what am I accused?"

Mademoiselle rapped his knuckles with her fan.

"*Voyons!* Have you finished with my hand?"

Instantly he turned back to her.

"I have lost count! Now I must begin again. One moment, Comte, I am much occupied!" Gravely he kissed each rosy finger a second time. "And one for the lovely whole. *Voilà!*"

"You are indeed a rogue," she told him. "For you care—not one jot!"

"If that were true I were a rogue beyond reprieve," he answered gaily.

"You don't deceive me, *le petit Philippe* . . . ! So sweet, so amiable, so great a flatterer—with no heart to lose!"

"Rumour hath it that 'tis already lost," smiled De Bergeret. "Eh, Philippe?"

"Lost an hundred times," mourned Philip, "and retrieved never!"

"Oh!" Mademoiselle started back in mock-anger. "Wretch that thou art, and so fickle! Rise! I'll no more of you!"

"Alack!" Philip came to his feet, and dusted his knee with his handkerchief. "I give you thanks, *mignonne,* 'twas very hard."

"But you do not say! How is she, la Pompadour?" cried De Salmy.

Philip pressed a hand to his forehead.

"La Pompadour? I do not know; I have forgotten. She has blue eyes, not black."

Mademoiselle promptly hid behind her fan.

Mr. Bancroft was staring at Philip as one in a trance. At that moment Philip looked his way. The grey eyes held no recognition and passed on.

"Good heavens!" exclaimed Bancroft. "'Tis never Mr. Jettan?"

"*Que lui dit-il?*" asked Mademoiselle, for Bancroft had spoken in English.

Philip bowed distantly.

"M'sieur?"

"You've not forgotten me? Bancroft?"

"Ah—Mr. Bancroft! I remember. Your servant, sir." He bowed again.

"Gad, I could scarce credit mine eyes! *Nom de Dieu!*"

"Aha, that I understand!" said Mademoiselle relievedly. "It is one of your friends, Philippe?" She smiled upon Mr. Bancroft with more warmth, and extended her hand. "*L'ami de Philippe*—ah, but you should have said!"

Mr. Bancroft was not elated at being classed as Philip's friend, but he bowed over Mademoiselle's hand with a good grace.

"I had no notion of finding him here, mademoiselle. The last time we met was—in a wood."

"Tell!" besought the lady.

Philip threw out his hands.

"Ah, no, *chérie!* That meeting was so disastrous to my vanity!"

"*Raison de plus*," decided Mademoiselle. "Tell me about it!"

"Mr. Bancroft and I had some slight difference in opinion which we settled in a wood. I was very easily worsted."

"*You?*" cried Mademoiselle. "Impossible!"

"On the contrary, *bien aimée*; I was, in those days, a very sorry spectacle, was I not, sir?"

"Not so long since," said Mr. Bancroft.

"Six months," nodded Philip, and turned to speak to the Comte de Saint-Dantin.

Mademoiselle was still incredulous.

"A sorry spectacle? Philippe?"

"I scent an intrigue," said a little Vicomte. "Clothilde, make him tell!"

"Of course," she said. "Philippe!"

Philip swung neatly round to face her.

"*Chère Clothilde?*"

"Come here! I want you to tell me what you mean by a sorry spectacle. If you refuse—*bien!* I shall ask Mr. Bancroft!"

"Oh, I'll give away no man's secrets!" simpered Bancroft.

Philip raised his eyeglass. He observed Mr. Bancroft dispassionately. Then he shrugged, and turned back to Clothilde.

"*Petite ange*, it's a sad tale. Six months ago I lived in the country, and I was a very churlish bumpkin. Then I was made to see the folly of my ways, and now—*me voici!*"

"I said that I scented an intrigue," said the Vicomte tranquilly.

"But wait, wait! *You* in the country, Philippe? You jest!"

68

"On my honour, no, *chérie*! I came to Paris to learn the ways of Polite Society."

"Six months ago?" De Bergeret was astonished. "It is your first visit? You learned all this in so short a time?"

"I have a natural aptitude," smiled Philip. "Now are you satisfied?"

"*Je n'en reviendrai jamais!*" Mademoiselle spoke emphatically. "*Jamais, jamais, jamais!*"

"I am not at all satisfied."

Philip cocked one eyebrow at the dainty Vicomte.

"What more would you have?"

"I would know of what like she is."

"She?"

"The lady to whom your heart is lost."

"That's an hundred she's," replied Philip airily. "And they are all different!"

"I dare swear I could enlighten M. de Ravel," drawled Bancroft.

All eyes turned his way. Philip seated himself beside Mademoiselle. He was smiling faintly.

"Proceed, *mon ami*. Who is this lady that I have forgotten?"

"Forgotten? Oh, come now, Jettan!"

Philip played with Clothilde's fan; he was still smiling, but the bright grey eyes that met Bancroft's held a challenge.

"If it transpired, m'sieur, that I had not forgotten it is possible that I might resent any liberties you or others thought to take with that lady's name," he said softly.

There was a sudden silence. No one could mistake the menacing note in Philip's smooth voice. Saint-Dantin made haste to fill the breach.

"The little Philippe is ready to fight us all, but it cannot be permitted. We'll not plague him, for he is very devilish when he is roused, I assure you!" He laughed easily and offered Bancroft snuff.

"He is very fastidious," sneered Bancroft.

M. le Comte closed his snuff-box and stepped back. He became politely bored.

"The subject grows somewhat tedious, I think. Mademoiselle, will you dance?"

Bancroft flushed. Mademoiselle sprang up.

"I am promised to Jules!" She nodded, smiling, to De Bergeret. Together they walked away from the little group.

Saint-Dantin linked arms with Philip.

"Come with me to the card-room, Philippe. Unless you wish to lead out la Salévier?" He nodded to where an opulent beauty stood.

"It's too fatiguing," said Philip. "I'll come."

"Who is he, the ill-disposed gentleman in pink?" inquired the Comte, when they were out of earshot.

"A creature of no importance," shrugged Philip.

"So I see. Yet he contrives to arouse your anger?"

"Yes," admitted Philip. "I do not like the colour of his coat."

"You may call upon me," said Saint-Dantin at once. "I do not like anything about him. He was here before—last year. His conversation lacks *finesse*. He is tolerated in London, *hein?*"

"I don't know. I trust not."

"*Hé, hé!* So he interfered between you and the lady?"

Philip withdrew his arm.

"Saint-Dantin!"

"Oh, yes, yes, I know! We all know that in the

background lurks—a lady! Else why your so chaste and cold demeanour?"

"Am I cold?"

"At the bottom, yes. Is it not so?"

"Certainly it is so. It's unfashionable to possess a heart."

"Oh, Philippe, thou art a rogue."

"So I have been told. Presumably because I am innocent of the slightest indiscretion. Curious. No one dubs you rogue who so fully merit the title. But I, whose reputation is spotless, am necessarily a wicked one and a deceiver. I shall write a sonnet on the subject."

"Ah, no!" begged Saint-Dantin in alarm. "Your sonnets are vile, Philippe! So let us have no more verse from you, I pray! All else you can do, but, *sacré nom de Dieu*, your verse—!"

"Alas!" sighed Philip, " 'tis my only ambition. I shall persevere."

Saint-Dantin paused, a hand on the curtain that shut off the card-room.

"Your only ambition, Philippe?"

"For the moment," answered Philip sweetly. "All things pall on one after a time."

"Save the greatest ambition?" Saint-Dantin's eyes were purely mischievous.

"You are as inquisitive as a monkey," said Philip, and propelled him into the card-room.

＊　　＊　　＊

"For how long has that fellow lorded it here?" asked Bancroft of his friend.

M. de Chambert flicked one great cuff with his handkerchief.

71

"Oh, some months! He is refreshing, is it not so? So young, so lovable."

"Lovable be damned!" said Bancroft.

De Chambert looked at him in surprise.

"You don't like our little Philippe?"

"No, I do not. Conceited young upstart!"

"Con—ah, but no! You misunderstand him! He pretends, and it is very amusing, but he is not conceited; he is just a *bébé*."

"Damn it, is he everyone's pet?"

"*C'est le dernier cri de Paris.* There are some who are jealous, naturally, but all who know him like him too much to be jealous."

"Jealous!" Bancroft snorted. "Jealous of that sprig!"

De Chambert cast him a shrewd glance.

"A word in your ear, m'sieu'! Do not speak your dislike too widely. *Le petit Philippe* has powerful friends. You will be frowned upon if you sneer at him."

Bancroft struggled for words.

"I'll—not conceal from you, De Chambert, that I've a grudge against your little Philippe. I punished him once before for impudence."

"Aha? I don't think you were well advised to do so again. He would have no lack of friends, and with a small-sword he is a veritable devil. It would not be wise to show your enmity, for you will meet him everywhere, and he is the ladies' darling. That says much, *hein*?"

"And when I saw him last," spluttered Bancroft, "he was clad in a coat I'd not give a lackey, and had as much conversation as a scarecrow!"

"Yes? I heard some talk of that. He is a marvel, our Philippe."

"Curse all marvels!" said Bancroft fervently.

CHAPTER VIII

In which Philip Delivers himself of a Rondeau

M. le Comte de Saint-Dantin gave a select dinner and card-party some few weeks after the coming of Mr. Bancroft. Only his chosen intimates were invited, and amongst them was Philip. At half-past five all the guests, save one, were assembled in the library, and Saint-Dantin was comparing his chronometer with the clock on the mantelpiece.

"Now what comes to Philippe?" he inquired of no one in particular. "Where is the child?"

"He was at the ball last night," said M. de Chatelin smoothing his ruffles. "He left early and in great haste." He raised his eyes and they were twinkling. "The pearl that hung from Madame de Marcherand's right ear inspired him and he fled."

"Fled? Why?"

"I believe, to compose a ballade in its honour."

Saint-Dantin flung up his hands.

"May the devil fly away with Philippe and his verse! I dare swear it's that that keeps him now."

Paul de Vangrisse turned his head.

"Do you speak of Philippe? I thought I heard his name?"

"But yes! Henri declares he is possessed of an inspiration for a ballade to Julie de Marcherand's pearl."

73

De Vangrisse came towards them, stiff silks rustling.

"Alas, it is too true. I visited him this morning and found him *en déshabillé*, clasping his brow. He seized on me and demanded a rhyme to some word which I have forgot. So I left him."

"Can no one convince Philippe that he is not a poet?" asked De Bergeret plaintively.

De Vangrisse shook his head.

"One may tell him that he is no swordsman, and no true *cavalier*; one may decry all his graces and he will laugh with one; but one may not say that he will never be a poet. He will not believe it."

"Oh, he believes it, *au fond*," answered Saint-Dantin. "It amuses him to pretend. Ah, here he is!"

Into the room came Philip, a vision in shades of yellow. He carried a rolled sheet of parchment, tied with an amber ribbon. He walked with a spring, and his eyes sparkled with pure merriment. He waved the parchment roll triumphantly.

Saint-Dantin went forward to greet him.

"But of a lateness, Philippe," he cried, holding out his hands.

"A thousand pardons, Louis! I was consumed of a rondeau until an hour ago."

"A rondeau?" said De Vangrisse. "This morning it was a ballade!"

"This morning? Bah! That was a year ago. Since then it has been a sonnet!"

"*A Dieu ne plaise!*" exclaimed Saint-Dantin devoutly.

"Of course," agreed Philip. "The theme demanded a rondeau. At three this afternoon I discovered that it was so. Did you come to see me this morning, Paul?"

"You asked me for a rhyme," De Vangrisse reminded him.

"So I did! A rhyme for *tout* and *fou,* and you gave me *chou!*"

"Whereupon you threw your wig at me, and I fled."

"*Chou!*" repeated Philip with awful scorn. "*Chou!*"

Gently but firmly Saint-Dantin took the parchment from him.

"You shall read it to us later," he promised. "But now you will dine."

"It goes well before meat," pleaded Philip.

He was answered by ribald protests.

"I'll not listen to your verse on an empty stomach," declared the Vicomte. "Belike I shall appreciate it when in my cups."

"You have no soul," said Philip sadly.

"But I have a stomach, *petit Anglais,* and it cries aloud for sustenance."

"I weep for you," said Philip. "Why do I waste my poetic gems upon you?"

Saint-Dantin took him by the elbow and led him to the door.

"*Parbleu, Philippe,* it's what we wish to know. You shall expound to us at dinner."

Midway through the meal the Vicomte remembered something. He nodded across the table to Philip, who was engaged in a lively and witty argument with De Bergeret.

"*A propos,* Philippe. Your so dear friend has been talking about you!"

"Which so dear friend?" asked Philip. "Jules, if you maintain in the face of my exposition that Jeanne de Fontenay can rival la Salévier in the matter of—"

"But attend!" insisted the Vicomte. "The Englishman—the Bancroft—*peste*, what a name for my tongue!"

Philip broke off in the middle of his discourse. His eyes gleamed in the candle-light.

"Bancroft? What does he say of me?"

"A great deal, if all I hear is true."

Philip set down his glass.

"Indeed! Now, what might you have heard, De Ravel?"

"It would appear that *ce cher* Bancroft feels no love for you, *mon pauvre*. If De Graune is to be believed, he resents your presence here. He says he has been deceived in you. It is all very sad."

"Yes," said Philip. He frowned. "Very sad. But what does he say?"

"He divulges your close-guarded secret," said the Vicomte solemnly.

"Oh!" Philip turned in his chair and leaned his elbows on the table. "It is possible that I shall have a word to say to M. Bancroft. Continue, Charles!"

"He speaks of a lady in 'Leetle Feeteldean' who has blue, blue eyes, and—"

"Shall we pass over her eyes?" smiled Philip.

"But certainly! Her hair—"

"And her hair? In fact, shall we pass over all her attractions?"

"He is very much in love," loudly whispered De Bergeret.

Philip flashed a smile at him.

"Very much, Jules. Proceed, Vicomte."

The Vicomte sipped his wine.

"M. Bancroft, he told of your—ah—infatuation. He described the lady—oh, fully!"

76

The thin lips were growing into a straight, smiling line, tightly compressed. Philip nodded.

"*Allons! Allons!*"

"Vicomte, does the gossip of the gaming-hells amuse you?" asked Saint-Dantin sharply.

But the Vicomte was a mischief-loving soul. He disregarded the rebuke.

"A pretty piece," he called her, "but no more than a simple country wench. By name—"

"Oh, have done!" exclaimed Saint-Dantin impatiently.

"But no!" Philip waved him aside. "I am very interested in what m'sieur has to say."

"By name, Cléone. We have it from M. Bancroft that she falls in love with him for his *beaux yeux* and his so charming manner."

"Ah!" Philip's chin sank into his cupped palms. "*Et puis?*"

"It is further recorded that one M. Philippe Jettan importuned her with his clumsy attentions, so that M. Bancroft was compelled to teach this M. Philippe a sharp lesson. And when one asks, 'What of the pretty Cléone?' he shrugs his shoulders and replies, very superbly, that he wearied of her as of all others."

Saint-Dantin's crisp voice cut into the sudden silence.

"Philippe, fill your glass. Paul here tells me of a pass he conceived in his duel with Mardry last month. A—"

"I will ask Paul to show me that pass," said Philip. He leant back in his chair and laughed softly. A moment later he had resumed his interrupted discussion with De Bergeret.

Afterwards Saint-Dantin took him aside.

"Philippe, I would not have had that happen at my table! Charles is incorrigible!"

"On the contrary, I am grateful to him," replied Philip. "I might not have heard else. Now I will shut that fellow's mouth."

"How?" asked Saint-Dantin blankly.

Philip made an imaginary pass in the air.

"Short of killing him," objected Saint-Dantin, "I don't see—"

"Kill him? Not I! I may count on you to—uphold me?"

"Of course. But what do you mean to do?"

"First I will reverse the table. I will punish him. Then I will assure him that my friends will espouse my cause if he again mentions my lady's name in public."

Saint-Dantin nodded.

"I'll vouch for those here to-night."

"Wait! Any mention of her name will be reported to me, and I shall send François to administer a little beating. It is well."

The Comte laughed outright.

"Oh, Philippe, thou art a young hot-head! Is this Cléone of so great account?"

Philip drew himself up.

"She is the lady whom I hope one day to make my wife."

"*Comment?* Your wife? Ah, *voyons! cela change l'affaire!* I did not know that. Stop his talk, by all means."

"It's what I am going to do," said Philip. "*Scélérat!*"

"With a vile taste for pink, *hein?* You'll call upon me?"

"If you please. And, I think, De Bergeret."

"Saint-Dantin, a wager!" called De Vangrisse. "What are you talking of so earnestly?"

"Of pink coats," answered Philip. "Oh, my rondeau! Where is it?"

"Devil take your rondeau!" cried the Vicomte. "Come and hazard a throw with me."

"A l'instant!" Philip untied the ribbon about his rondeau and spread out the parchment. "I insist that you shall listen to this product of my brain!" He mounted a chair amid derisive cheers, and bowed right and left in mock solemnity. "To the Pearl that Trembles in her Ear."

> "Cette petite perle qui tremblotte
> Au bout ton oreille, et qui chuchotte
>   Je ne sais quoi de tendre et de malin.
>   A l'air à la fois modeste et coquin,
> Si goguenarde est elle et si dévote.
>
> A regarder c'est toute une gavotte
> Où l'on s'avance, se penche, et pivote,
>   Lors que tu branles d'un mouvement fin
>   Cette petite perle.
>
> C'est une étoile dans le ciel qui flotte—
> Un vif éclair qui luit dans une grotte—
>   Un feu follet qui hors de mon chemin
>   M' attire, m' éblouit, m' égare—"

Philip paused for his final effect. Arose Saint-Dantin, and like a flash interjected:

>   "Enfin,
> Elle 'm embête—saperlipopOtte!—
>   Cette petite perle."

Outraged, Philip threw the parchment at his head.

CHAPTER IX

Mr. Bancroft is Enraged

"Philippe, do you go to De Farraud's to-night?" asked De Bergeret suddenly. He was lounging on the couch in Philip's room, watching Philip adjust his patches.

"De Farraud's? I'd not thought of it. Whom shall I meet there?"

"Your very obedient," said De Bergeret, flourishing his hat.

"The prospect does not entice me," answered Philip. "No, don't retort! Don't speak. Don't move!" He leaned forward, shifting a candle to throw its light on his face, and frowned at his reflection. The white hand that held the haresfoot wavered an instant, and then alighted at the corner of his mouth. Philip sat back, studying the effect.

"Whom else shall I meet, Jules?"

"The usual people, I fancy. And some others, no doubt."

"De Farraud's friends are so very mixed," deplored Philip. "Do you suppose that De Chambert will be present?"

"Nothing is more certain," yawned De Bergeret. "But it will be amusing, and the play will be high, which is all that matters."

"But De Chambert wears puce small-clothes," objected Philip.

"Does he? *Mordieu*, I'd like to see that! Puce small-clothes, forsooth! And what does our Philippe wear?"

Philip glanced lovingly down at his pearl-grey breeches.

"Grey, and palest pink, with lacings of silver." He slipped out of his gaily-hued robe, and stood up.

De Bergeret levelled his eyeglass at him.

"*Parbleu, Philippe!* Grey lace!"

Philip shook out his ruffles.

"A sweet conceit, *hein?* But wait! François, my vest!"

His valet brought it, and helped Philip to put it on. It was a very exquisite confection of pink and silver brocade.

De Bergeret was interested.

"I'll swear you designed that, Philippe! Now for the coat!"

When Philip had at last succeeded in entering into the coat it was some ten minutes later. François stepped back, panting; Philip arranged his sword to his satisfaction.

"A careless sprinkling of rubies, *hein?* One in the cravat, one here, another in my wig. And on my fingers, so . . . !"

"Perfect!" applauded de Bergeret. "*Tonnerre de Dieu*, pink humming-birds on your stockings!"

François beamed and clasped his hands, gazing in rapt admiration at Philip's startlingly clocked legs.

Philip laughed.

"Do they please your artistic soul, Jules? And are they to be wasted on De Farraud? I had intended to go to the Saint-Clamond rout, where I know I shall meet Clothilde. Come with me!"

De Bergeret shook his head.

"I promised De Vangrisse I'd be at De Farraud's some time to-night. Forget the lovely Clothilde, Philippe. Bethink you, your so dear friend Bancroft will come to Farraud's in De Chambert's train!"

Philip was fixing a long ruby ear-ring in his right ear, but he stopped suddenly, and looked over his shoulder at De Bergeret.

"*Comment?*"

"Why, you leap to my bait!" said De Bergeret, amused. "I thought you could not resist so great an attraction!"

Philip fixed the ruby and swept round for his cloak and hat.

"Faith, that can I not. I come, Jules, I come! François, thou rogue, my snuff-box! Would that he may be wearing that salmon-pink! François, my cane! Jules, you are sitting on my cloak! *Sangdieu!* my new cloak!" He swept De Bergeret off the coat, and shook out the soft, rose-lined folds. "God be praised, it is unhurt!" With a deft movement he swung it over his shoulders and fastened it. "My hat! Jules, what think you of my hat?"

"A grey hat! Philippe, what an audacity! You are really coming to De Farraud's?"

"To meet the so dear M. Bancroft. *En avant, Jules!*"

De Bergeret went to the glass.

"Cultivate a more restful manner, *mon petit!* I am not to be hurried. Do you like this mixture of violet and cream?"

"I like everything you have on, even the so badly arranged cravat! I am consumed with impatience! Come!"

"But why? Are you hasting to see the unspeakable Bancroft?"

"But yes! Whom else? I will explain *en route.*"

De Bergeret suffered himself to be led to the door.

"Philippe, it is not *convenable* to display such enthusiasm. Languor is now the fashion."

"I am a fashion unto myself, then. I am an original. And I go to call out M. Bancroft!"

De Bergeret stopped short.

"What! A brawl? No, then, I'll not come!"

"A brawl? Is it possible? I shall conduct the affair with great *douceur*, I assure you! You and Saint-Dantin are to be my seconds."

"*Miséricorde!* Philippe, you become more and more tiresome!" expostulated his friend. "Why must you fight this fellow?"

"An old quarrel—the settling of an unpaid score! *Allons!*"

* * *

"Oh, the devil," muttered Bancroft.

"*Où donc?*" inquired Le Vallon, who was sitting next him and who understood English.

Bancroft shot an angry glance towards the door. Le Vallon turned to see what had excited his wrath.

Talking to De Farraud, with many quick gestures and smiles, was Philip. He had just arrived, and he was apologizing for his lateness, throwing all the blame on De Bergeret, who accepted it meekly.

"Oh, the little Englishman!" said Le Vallon scornfully. "Always late, always eccentric. And grey lace! What an affectation!"

Philip cast a swift glance round the room. His eyes rested an instant on Bancroft's face, then they passed on. Two or three men called to him, and he presently went to dice with De Vangrisse. But when Le Vallon left Bancroft to join a faro group, Philip swept up his dice, and with a laughing word to De Vangrisse, promising to return, he walked over to Bancroft's table, and sat down in Le Vallon's chair with a swirl of his full skirts.

Bancroft was about to rise. Astonished at Philip's sudden advent, he sank back again.

"To what do I owe this honour?" he demanded.

Philip dealt out the cards.

"I will tell you. A hand of piquet? You will declare?" Bancroft sorted his hand rather sullenly. Not until he had declared and played his card did Philip speak again. Then he took the trick and leant forward.

"It comes to my ears that you have been bandying a certain lady's name about Paris in a way that does not please me. You understand, yes?"

"What the devil is it to you?" cried Bancroft, crimson-faced.

" 'Sh, sh! Not so loud, if you please! Go on playing! I am informed that you speak of this lady as a pretty piece! It is not how I will have you speak of her. Also, you say that she fell in love with you *en désespéré*. *Eh bien*, I say that you lie in your throat!"

"Sir!"

"*Doucement, doucement*. Further, I say that if so be you again mention this lady's name in public I shall send my lackeys to punish you. It is understood?"

"You—you—you impudent young cockerel! I shall know how to answer this! What's Cleone to you, eh?"

The pleasant smile died. Philip leaned forward.

"That name I will not have spoken, m'sieur. Strive to bear it in mind. I have many friends, and they will tell me if you speak of the lady when I am not by. And of the rest I have warned you."

"Ye can understand this, Mr. Jettan—I'll speak of her how and when I like!"

Philip shrugged.

"You talk foolishly. There is no question of refusal to comply with my wishes. If I so please I can make Paris ve-ry uncomfortable for you. You know that, I think."

Bancroft was speechless with rage.

"There is another matter," continued Philip amiably. "Once before I had occasion to complain of your manner. I do so again. And I find the colour of your ribbons most distasteful to mine eye."

Bancroft sprang up, his chair grating on the polished floor.

"Perhaps you'll have the goodness to name your friends, sir?" he choked.

Philip bowed.

"This time, yes. It is a little debt I have to pay. M. le Comte de Saint-Dantin and M. de Bergeret will act for me. Or De Vangrisse yonder, or M. le Duc de Vally-Martin."

"The first named will suffice," snapped Bancroft. "My friends will wait on them as soon as may be." With that he flounced away to the other end of the room.

Philip walked back to De Vangrisse and perched on the arm of his chair.

De Bergeret cast his dice and nodded to Philip.

"The deed is done?"

"Most satisfactorily," answered Philip. "Throw, Paul, you can beat that."

"Not I! Jules has the devil's own luck to-night. If it is not an impertinence, are you to meet M. Bancroft?"

"Of course. Oh, *pestel*"—as De Vangrisse cast his dice.

"What did I tell you? May I second you?"

"A thousand thanks, Paul. But Saint-Dantin and Jules have consented to act for me."

"Well, I shall come as a spectator," said De Vangrisse. "Jules, another hundred! I'll not be beaten by you!"

Le Vallon, who had watched the brief encounter between his friend and Philip with great curiosity, now edged across to where Bancroft was standing.

Bancroft turned.

"Come apart a moment," he said. His voice was still trembling with passion. He and Le Vallon drew near to the window.

"You saw that damned fellow come up to me just now?"

"But yes! I watched very closely. What did he want with you?"

"He came to impose his will—his will!—on mine. Curse his impudence!"

"Why? What did he say?" asked Le Vallon inquisitively.

Bancroft did not answer.

"I want you to act for me," he said abruptly. "He—insulted me, and I've sworn to teach him a lesson."

Le Vallon drew back a little.

"What? You seek to kill him? Kill *le petit Anglais?*" His tone was dubious.

"No, not quite that. I've no wish for trouble. He has too many friends. I'll teach him to leave me alone!"

"Oh, yes! But . . ." Le Vallon pursed his lips.

"But what?" barked Bancroft.

"It is said that he is a not-to-be-despised swordsman. He pinked Armand de Sedlamont with great ease."

"Pooh!" said Bancroft. "Six months ago——"

"I know, I know, but he has changed."

Bancroft scowled.

"Well, will you act for me or not?"

Le Vallon drew himself up.

"M'sieur, I do not entirely appreciate your manner."

Bancroft laughed uneasily.

"Oh, come, Le Vallon! Don't take offence! That puppy has so annoyed me that I can scarce keep my temper. Where's De Chambert?"

"Playing at lansquenet with De Farraud. And I think we had best mingle with the others. I do not care to appear conspicuous."

Bancroft caught at his arm.

"But you will second me?"

"I shall be honoured," bowed Le Vallon. "And I hope you will succeed in showing my fine gentleman his place."

Later in the evening Saint-Dantin sauntered over to where Philip sat, perched on the edge of the table, toasting some of his friends. Saint-Dantin joined the gathering and laid a hand on Philip's shoulder. Philip, who was drinking, choked.

"*Malédiction!* Oh, 'tis you, Louis! What now?"

"There is a rumour that you go to fight *ce cher* Bancroft, Philippe."

"Already?" Philip was startled. "Who told you?"

"*Personne.*" Saint-Dantin smiled. "It is whispered here and there. And Bancroft looks so black at you. It's true?"

"Of course it's true! Did I not say I should do it? His seconds are to wait upon you and Jules."

"How very fatiguing!" sighed Saint-Dantin. "But quite amusing. One jubilates. Bancroft is not at all liked. He is so *entreprenant*. An I mistake not, you will have an audience," he chuckled.

"What?" Philip gripped his wrist. "I won't have an audience!"

Saint-Dantin blinked, loosening the clasp on his wrist.

"*Pas si éclatant*, Philippe," he said. "You twist and turn like a puppet on wires! I only know that at least five here to-night swear they'll see the fight."

"But it is monstrous!" objected Philip. "I forbid you to divulge the whereabouts of the meeting."

"Oh, *entendu*! But the secret will out."

"How am I to keep a steady wrist with a dozen ogling fools watching?" demanded Philip.

"You must keep it steady," said De Chatelin. "My money's for you, *petit Anglais*!"

Philip looked genuinely perturbed.

"Henri, it is iniquitous! It is not a public exhibition that I engage in! One would say we were gladiators!"

"*Reste tranquille*," grinned De Vangrisse. "We are all backing you, *mon petit*."

"I trust you'll not forget to inform His Majesty of the rendezvous," said Philip, resorting to bitter sarcasm. "And have you engaged a fiddler to enliven the meeting?"

"*Philippe se fâche*," teased De Chatelin. "Quiet, little fighting cock!"

"I shall write an ode!" threatened Philip direfully.

"Ah no, that is too much!" cried De Vangrisse with feeling.

"And I shall read it to you before I engage. Well?"

"It is a heavy price to pay," answered Paul, "but not too heavy for entertainment."

CHAPTER X

In which a Letter is Read

Cleone sat on a stool at Sir Maurice's knee and sighed. So did Sir Maurice, and knew that they sighed for the same thing.

"Well, my dear," he said, trying to speak cheerfully, "how is your mamma?"

"The same as ever, I thank you," answered Cleone.

Sir Maurice patted her head.

"And how is little Cleone?"

"Oh, sir, can you ask? I am very well," she said, with great sprightliness. "And you?"

Sir Maurice was more honest.

"To tell the truth, my dear, I miss that young scamp."

Cleone played with his fingers, her head bent.

"Do you, sir? He should be home again ere long. Do you—do you yet know where he is?"

"No. That does not worry me. My family does not write letters."

"Mr. Tom—has not told you, I suppose?"

"No. I've not seen Tom for some time. . . . The boy has been away six months now. Gad, but I'd like to see him walk in at that door!"

Cleone's head sank a little lower.

"Do you think—harm could have come to him, sir?"

"No. Else had I heard. Faith, it's our own fault, Cleone, and we are grumbling!"

"I never—"

"My dear, don't pretend to me! Do you think I don't know?"

Cleone was silent.

"We sent Philip to acquire polish. Heaven knows what has happened to him! Would you care greatly if he returned—without the polish, child?"

"No!" whispered Cleone.

"Nor should I. Strange! But I should prefer it, I confess."

"Do you think—do you think he—he will be—very elegant, Sir Maurice?"

He smiled.

"I fear not, Cleone. Can you see our Philip tricked up in town clothes, apeing town ways?"

"N—no."

There was silence for a few minutes.

"Sir Maurice."

"My dear?"

"Mamma has a letter from my aunt, Lady Malmerstoke."

"So? And what does she say therein?"

"She—she wants me to go to her for the season."

Sir Maurice looked down at her.

"And you are going?"

"I don't—know. I—do not wish to leave you, sir."

"That is very kind of you, child. But I'd not have you stay for my sake."

"It's no such thing, sir. I do not want to go."

"Why, Cleone, not for the season? Think of the balls and the routs."

"I don't—care about it." It was a forlorn little voice, and Sir Maurice patted her hand again.

"Tut-tut, my love!"

Another silence.

"I do not think it is very kind in Philip to stay away from you for so long a time," said Cleone wistfully.

"You forget, dear. I sent him. He is but obeying me."

"And—and me."

Sir Maurice found nothing to say to that.

"Was I—perhaps—very wicked —to—to—do what he said—I did?"

"What was that, Cleone?"

"Th—throw away—an honest man's love for—for —oh, you know the things he said!"

"Silly young fool! You gave him his just deserts, Cleone. And you may vouch for it that he will be back here at your feet in a very short while."

Cleone glanced up through her lashes.

"Do you really think so?" she asked eagerly.

"Of course I do!" he answered stoutly.

Just then a bell clanged somewhere in the distance. Cleone jumped up and ran to the window which looked out on the avenue. She tip-toed, craning her neck to see who stood in the porch.

"Why, it is Sir Harold Bancroft!" she exclaimed.

"Plague take him, then!" said Sir Maurice, disagreeably. "I can't stand the fellow or his sprig of a son!"

Cleone blushed and continued to stand with her back to the room until footsteps sounded along the passage, and the door opened to admit the visitor.

Sir Maurice rose.

"Give ye good den, Bancroft. It's good of you to come to visit me this cold day."

Bancroft wrung the thin hand, pressing Sir Maurice's rings into his fingers. He bowed jerkily to the curtseying Cleone, and blurted forth his errand.

"'Tis a joke I must have you share! 'Twill be the death of you, I vow. You knew my son was in Paris?"

Sir Maurice put forward a chair.

"Really? No, I did not know."

"Well, he is. And"—a chuckle escaped him—"so is yours!"

"Oh!" It was a smothered exclamation from Cleone. Sir Maurice smiled.

"I guessed as much," he said, quite untruthfully. "Have you news from Henry?"

"No, not I! But I've a letter from an old friend of mine—Satterthwaite. Do ye know him?"

Sir Maurice shook his head. Having seen his guest into a chair, he sat down on the couch, and beckoned Cleone to his side.

"No. He, too, is in Paris?"

"Ay. Now wait while I find the letter! You'll split o' laughter when you've heard me read it!" He rummaged in his capacious pockets, and drew forth two or three crumpled sheets. These he spread out, and proceeded to find the place.

"'I trust . . .' No, that's not it! 'We are' . . . Hum, hum, hum! Ah, here we have it! Just listen to this!" He held the parchment close to his nose and began to read:

"'. . . Whom should I meet but your boy, Henry! I had no notion he was in Paris, or I should have sought him out, you may depend. The manner of my meeting with him was most singular, as you will agree, and it is the more interesting as the occasion affords the subject for the latest joke of Paris, nay, I may almost say scandal, though to be sure I mean not our meeting,

94

but that which I am about to relate. . . .' A bit involved, that," remarked Bancroft, frowning.

"Not at all," said Sir Maurice. "I understand perfectly."

"Well, it's more than I do! However: 'I came upon Moosoo de Château-Banvau the other day . . .'"

"Château-Banvau!"

"Eh? Do ye know him?"

"Do I know him! As I know my brother!"

"Fancy! There's a coincidence! But there's more to come! Where was I? Oh, yes—'came upon Moosoo de Château-Banvau the other day and found him in great amusement, which he offered me to share, and the which I agreed to. He propounded me the joke that we were to see, and one in which his *protégé*, a Mr. Philip Jettan, was the part cause of and your son, Henry, the other!' Gad, that's a fine sentence! Are ye listening to me, Jettan?"

There was no need to ask that question. Both his auditors had their whole attention fixed on him. Satisfied, he continued: "'This young Jettan is, so says the Marquis, the craze of Fashionable Paris, the ladies' darling'—do ye hear that now?—'and the maddest young scamp that you could wish for. Then the Marquis further told me that Henry was in Paris and engaged to fight a duel with this Jettan.'"

"Oh, heavens!" cried Cleone.

"Ye may well say so, my dear! Now, wait a while—the joke's against me, I confess, but I had to tell you—'The cause whereof, it is rumoured, is some lady whom both are enamoured of, some French wench, I think.'"

Cleone was rigid. Her fingers tightened unconsciously on Sir Maurice's arm.

"'Jettan being a great favourite among the young

95

sparks here, they all, having got wind of the affair, combined among themselves, laying wagers about the fight, the most of the money being laid on Jettan, as I hear. Then to bait him, or whatnot, they conspired to be present at the meeting despite Jettan's protests. The Marquis laughed mightily here, and said that Jettan threatened to read them an ode should they appear, which he seemed to find vastly entertaining on account of some joke or other concerning Jettan's poetry.'"

"Philip's *poetry* . . . ?" said Sir Maurice faintly. "Proceed, Bancroft."

"Ay, wait a bit! Here we are: 'The Marquis was going to be present, having heard of the rumour and swore to take me along with him. The which I did consent to, as you may imagine. Well, we come out to Neuilly in due course at half-after eight one morning, and mighty cold it was, but that's neither here nor there. There we found a fair gathering of young rakes with their horses or chariots, some half dozen in all, laying wagers and all mightily amused. And, stap me, if there was not a fiddler scraping away as if his life depended on it. Soon after we were come, up drives a coach and out jumps three men, the first in great disorder at finding so many there assembled. This was Jettan, and prodigious elegant and finicky he was, too, all patched and painted, and tricked up in velvets and silks and I don't know what. He fell into a great rage, though he was laughing half the time, and, indeed, 'twas a ridiculous situation, and he could scarce help but to be tickled by it. He turns to his seconds and rates them, but they were too amused to do aught but to hold their sides. Then young Jettan orders us all off and especially begs the Marquis to exert his influence, which he would not do. Then Jettan, appealed to us to withdraw, whereat they were all the more entertained, and adjured him to *se taire*, as they call it, calling him *petit Philippe* and the like. Then Jettan started to laugh himself and pulls out a roll of parchment from his pocket, and was for declaiming some ode he had writ, but that three of them took it from him. Then he says, "At least, send that damned fiddler away!" and they replied, "All in good time," but 'twas himself had asked for him. Before he could say more, which he was about to do, up comes another coach, and out gets your boy, Henry, and his seconds. When they saw what was toward they were mightily put out, as you may imagine, and, indeed, Henry was white and purple with rage, saying this was an insult and he was not to be so mocked, and the like. His seconds spoke apart with young Jettan's, and I give you my word, they were dancing with fury, at least one was, but the little one seemed more entertained. Then up comes Jettan, very solemn and dignified, and bows to Henry. "I ask you to believe, moosoo," says he, "that this is none of my designing. I desire," says he, "to offer you my apologies for my friends' ill-timed pleasantry." Henry could scarce mouth forth a word, so enraged was he, and was for retiring at once, saying that he had borne much, but this was too much. The fiddler was ordered to stop his scraping now, and the onlookers all vowed they had come with serious intent to watch the fight, and would not go until they had done so. Jettan offers to meet Henry another day, when and where he will, but I could see Henry was burning to run him through. "Since we are here," says he, "let us go on with it. I await your convenience," he says, and, "I thank you," replies Jettan and stands back. Henry's seconds were all for retiring, but he'd have none of it, and bids them go to and choose the ground. At last all was prepared, and the two stripped off their coats and vests. Everyone was becomingly sober now, and, indeed, mighty anxious for young Jettan, who is the smaller of the two, and Henry looking murder as he was. Henry fought devilish hard, and, indeed, is a cunning fencer, as you no doubt apprehend, but young Jettan was like a bit of quicksilver, in and out with his sword most finicky and dainty. Soon we saw that Henry was no match for him at all, and, indeed, could have been run through the body a score of times, Jettan playing with him very pretty to see, but I was sore distressed to see Henry so put to it. He gave Jettan but the faintest scratch, and before we knew what was to do, there was Henry reeling back and his sword on the ground. At which Jettan bows very polite, and but a mite out of breath, and picks up the sword and hands it to Henry. Henry was for continuing, and a brave lad he is, but the seconds would have none of it, and 'twas all over. "I trust you are satisfied, sir?" says Jettan. "Satisfied be damned!" pants Henry, clutching at his shoulder. "Of the other matter between us," says Jettan, "I can only counsel you to remember, for I meant what I said." Then he walks off and we rode away.'" Bancroft stopped. "I saw the joke was against me. What do ye think of that, Sir Maurice?"

Sir Maurice drew a deep breath.

"My God, I would I had been there!" he said fervently.

"Ay, 'twould have been a fine sight, I vow! But did ye ever hear the like of it? Philip and the petticoats, eh? These lads, Sir Maurice! These lads! Satterthwaite says he writes madrigals and what-not to the ladies' eyelashes!" Bancroft went off into a long chuckle.

"And so ruffled my young hothead, who had always a way with the petticoats!"

Cleone rose and walked to the window. She opened it, cooling her hot cheeks. And there she stayed, seated on the low couch that ran under the window, until Bancroft finally took his departure.

When Sir Maurice returned from seeing his guest out of the house, he found her pale again, and very stiff.

"Ahem!" said Sir Maurice. Then, brusquely: "Pack o' lies!"

"Do you think so?" said Cleone hopefully.

"Of course I do! The boy is but doing what I told him to do—acquiring polish and *savoir faire* with your sex, my dear."

Cleone sprang up.

"You told him to—oh, how could you, sir?"

"My dear, it's less than nothing, I dare swear. But Philip worsting Bancroft like that! Philip the pet of Society! Gad, I never hoped for this!"

"Nor I," said Cleone bitterly. "And—and 'tis my own—f-fault—for—s-sending him away—s-so c-cruelly, but—but—oh, how *dare* he?"

Sir Maurice was silent.

"He—he—I thought he—" she broke off, biting her lip. After a slight pause she spoke again, with would-be lightness. "I—do you know, I think I shall go to my aunt after all?"

"Will you, my dear?" said Sir Maurice.

That evening he was moved to write to his brother, an infrequent proceeding. The outcome of that letter was a brief note from Tom, which reached Philip a week later.

"Dear Nephew,—The Devil's in it now and no Mis-

99

take. Old Satterthwaite was Present at your crazy
Duel, and has writ the whole Tale to Harry Bancroft,
who, curse him for an interfering old Fool, read it to
your Father and Cleone. The Tale is that you and B.
quarrelled over some French Minx, which may be
True for all I know. In any Case, Cleone is monstrous
put out, and Comes to Towne to her Aunt, old Sally
Malmerstoke. Maurice writes me this and demands
your Return, being Upset for the Girl's sake, but se-
cretly Delighted at the Story, if I read his Letter
aright. Do as you please, dear Boy, but I warn you,
Cleone is in the Mood for any Madness, as is the way
when a Maid thinks herself slighted. And she is a Prodigious pretty Chit. My love to Château-Banvau and
to Yr Self.—Tom."

CHAPTER XI

Philip Astonishes his Uncle

Thomas, deep in the latest copy of the *Rambler*, was aroused by the sound of wheels drawing up outside the house. He rose and stretched himself, wondering who could choose such a day wherein to visit him. He strolled to the window and peered out into the foggy street. He was surprised to see, not a light town-chariot, but a large travelling coach, top-heavy with baggage, and drawn by four steaming horses. As he watched, the door of the vehicle was thrown open and a slight gentleman sprang out, not waiting for the steps to be let down. He was muffled in a many-caped overcoat of Parisian cut, and shining leather boots were on his feet. Tom was puzzled. Then, from out the coach, issued two other men, evidently servants, the one small and wiry, the other lank and cadaverous. Both seemed depressed. The man in the well-cut cloak waved his hands at them and appeared to shoot forth a number of instructions. The little man, scarcely visible beneath the band-boxes that he carried, nodded, shivered, and rounded on the lean man. Then the man in the cloak turned, and ran up the steps to Tom's front door. A long bell-peal sounded through the house.

Tom walked to the fire and stood with his back to it. Possibly this was his friend Mainwaring come to

101

visit him, but why did he bring so much baggage? Tom rather hoped that the unknown guest had come to his house in mistake for another's.

But a quick tread came across the hall and the door of the library was swept open. Hat in hand, the visitor stood before Tom, bowing.

"Revered uncle, I kiss your hands!" And he proceeded to do so.

"God ha' mercy, it's Philip!" gasped Tom. "I never expected you for another week, lad!"

Philip tossed his hat and gloves on to the table and wriggled out of his cloak.

"I am *de trop,* no?"

"Never in your life!" Tom assured him. "Stand up, child, and let me look at you!" Then, as Philip clicked his heels together and faced him, laughing, his eyes widened, and his lips formed a soundless whistle. "By the Lord Harry, Philip, it's marvellous! How could you do it in six months—!"

Philip rustled over to the fire and stooped, warming his hands.

"Fog, cold, damp! Brrh! The unspeakable climate! Tom, it is permitted that I stay with you until I find an abode?"

With difficulty his uncle withdrew his gape from Philip's claret-coloured coat of fine cloth, laced with gold.

"Can you ask? Stay as long as you will, lad, you're a joy to behold!"

"*Merci du compliment!*" smiled Philip. "You perhaps admire the mixture of claret and biscuit as I wear it?"

Tom's eyes travelled down to the creaseless biscuit-coloured small-clothes.

102

"Ay. I admire everything. The boots most of all. The boots—Philip, where did you obtain them?"

Philip glanced carelessly down at his shapely leg.

"They were made for me. Me, I am not satisfied with them. I shall give them to François."

"Give them to François?" cried his uncle. "Ye wicked boy! Where is the fellow?"

"He and Jacques are struggling with my baggage and Moggat." He stretched out a detaining hand as Tom started forward to the door. "Ah, do not disturb yourself! I have spoken with *ce bon* Moggat, and all is well. He will arrange everything."

Tom came back.

"He will be in a frenzy, Philip! All that baggage!"

"All—that baggage?" Philip spoke with uplifted brows. "It has arrived?" He went to the window and looked out. "But no, not yet."

"B—but—is there more to come?" asked Tom.

"But of course! The bulk follows me."

Tom sat down weakly.

"And you who six months ago thought yourself rich in the possession of three coats."

Philip came back to the fire. He made a little grimace of distaste.

"Those far-off days! That is ended—completely!"

Tom cast him a shrewd glance.

"What, all of it? Cleone?"

"Ah!" Philip smiled. "That is—another—matter. I have to thank you for your letter, Tom."

"It brought you back?"

"*En partie.* She is here?"

"Ay, with Sally Malmerstoke. She is already noticed. Sally takes her everywhere. She is now looked for—and courted." His eyes twinkled.

103

"Oho!" said Philip. He poured out a glass of burgundy from the decanter that stood on a small table. "So she is furious with me, yes?"

"So I believe. Satterthwaite wrote that you and Bancroft fought over the fair name of some French lass. Did you?"

Philip sipped his wine.

"Not a whit. 'Twas her own fair name, *à vrai dire.*"

"Oh! You'll tell her that, of course?"

"Not at all."

Tom stared.

"What then? Have you some deep game in mind, Philip?"

"Perhaps. Oh, I don't know! I thank her for reforming me, but, being human, I am hurt and angry! *Le petit Philippe se fâche,*" he said, smiling suddenly. "He would see whether it is himself she loves, or—a painted puppet. It's foolish, but what would you?"

"So you are now a painted puppet?" said Tom politely.

"What else?"

"Dear me!" said Tom, and relapsed into profound meditation.

"I want to have her love me for—myself, and not for my clothes, or my airs and graces. It's incomprehensible?"

"Not entirely," answered Tom. "I understand your feelings. What's to do?"

"Merely my baggage," said Philip, with another glance towards the window. "It is the coach that you hear."

"No, not that." Tom listened. Voices raised in altercation sounded in the hall.

Philip laughed.

"That is the inimitable François. I do not think that Moggat finds favour in his eyes."

"I'll swear he does not find favour in Moggat's eyes! Who is the other one?"

"Jacques, my groom and *homme à tout faire.*"

"Faith, ye've a retinue!"

"What would you?" shrugged Philip. He sat down opposite his uncle, and stretched his legs to the fire. "Heigh-ho! I do not like this weather."

"Nor anyone else. What are you going to do, now that you have returned?"

"Who knows? I make my bow to London Society, I amuse myself a little—ah yes! and I procure a house."

"Do you make your bow to Cleone?"

An impish smile danced into Philip's eyes.

"I present myself to Cleone—as she would have had me. A drawling, conceited, and mincing fop. Which I am not, believe me!"

Tom considered him.

"No, you're not. You don't drawl."

"I shall drawl," promised Philip. "And I shall be very languid."

"It's the fashion, of course. You did not adopt it?"

"It did not entice me. I am *le petit sans repos,* and *le Petit Philippe au Cœur Perdu,* and *petit original. Hé hé,* I shall be homesick! It is inevitable."

"Are you so much at home in Paris?" asked Tom, rather surprised. "You liked the Frenchies?"

"Liked them! Could I have disliked them?"

"I should have thought it possible—for you. Did you make many friends?"

"*A revendre!* They took me to their bosoms."

"Did they indeed! Who do you count amongst your intimates?"

"Saint-Dantin—you know him?"

"I've met him. Tall and dark?"

"Ay. Paul de Vangrisse, Jules de Bergeret, Henry de Chatelin—oh, I can't tell you! They are all charming!"

"And the ladies?"

"Also charming. Did you ever meet Clothilde de Chaucheron, or Julie de Marcherand? *Ah, voilà ce qui fait ressouvenir!* I count that *rondeau* one of my most successful efforts. You shall hear it some time or other."

"That *what?*" ejaculated Tom, sitting upright in his surprise.

"A *rondeau*: 'To the Pearl that Trembles in Her Ear'. I would you could have seen it."

"Which? The *rondeau?*"

"The pearl, man! The *rondeau* you shall most assuredly see."

"Merciful heaven!" gasped Tom. "A *rondeau!* Philip —poet! *Sacr-ré mille petits cochons!*"

"Monsieur dines at home this evening?" asked François.

Philip sat at his dressing-table, busy with many pots and his face. He nodded.

"The uncle of Monsieur receives, without doubt?"

"A card-party," said Philip, tracing his eyebrows with a careful hand.

François skipped to the wardrobe and flung it open. With a finger to his nose he meditated aloud.

"The blue and silver . . . *un peu trop soigné.* The orange . . . *peu convenable.* The purple . . . the purple . . . *essayons!*"

Philip opened the rouge-jar.

"The grey I wore at De Flaubert's last month."

François clapped a hand to his head.

"*Ah, sot!*" he apostrophised himself. "*Voilà qui est tres bien.*" He dived into the wardrobe emerging presently with the required dress. He laid it on the bed, stroking it lovingly, and darted away to a large chest. From it he brought forth the pink and silver waistcoat that De Bergeret had admired, and the silver lace. Then he paused. "*Les bas . . . ? Les bas aux oiseaux-mouches . . . où sont-ils?*" He peered into a drawer, turning over neat piles of stockings. A convulsion of fury seemed to seize him, and he sped to the door. "Ah, *sapristi! Coquin! Jacques!*"

In answer to his frenzied call came the cadaverous one, shivering. François seized him by the arm and shook him.

"Thou misbegotten son of a toad!" he raved. "Where is the small box I bade you guard with your life! Where is it, I say. Thou——"

"I gave it into your hands," said Jacques sadly. "Into your hands, your very hands, in this room here by the door! I swear it."

"Swear it? What is it to me, you swear? I say I have not seen the box! At Dover, what did I do? *Nom d'un nom,* did I not say to you, lose thy head sooner than that box?" His voice rose higher and higher. "And now, where is it?"

"I tell you I gave it you! It is this bleak country that has warped your brain. Never did the box leave my hands until I gave it into yours!"

"And I say you did not! *Saperlipopette,* am I a fool that I should forget? Now listen to what you have done! You have lost the stockings of Monsieur! By your incalculable stupidity, the stupidity of a pig, an ass——"

"*Sacré nom de Dieu!* Am I to be disturbed by your shrieking?" Philip had flung down the haresfoot. He

107

slewed round in his chair. "Shut the door! Is it that you wish to annoy my uncle that you shout and scream in his house?" His voice was thunderous.

François spread out his hands.

"M'sieur, I ask pardon! It is this *âne*, this careless *gaillard*—"

"*Mais, m'sieur!*" protested Jacques. "It is unjust; it is false!"

"*Ecoutez donc, m'sieur!*" begged François, as the stern grey eyes went from his face to that of the unhappy Jacques. "It is the band-box that contains your stockings—the stockings *aux oiseaux-mouches*! Ah, would that I had carried it myself! Would that—"

"Would that you would be quiet!" said Philip severely. "If either of you have lost those stockings . . ." He paused, and once more his eyes travelled from one to the other. "I shall seek another valet."

François became tearful.

"Ah, no, no, m'sieur! It is this *imbécile*, this *crapaud*—"

"*M'sieu', je vous implore*—"

Philip pointed dramatically across the room. Both men looked fearfully in the direction of that accusing finger.

"Ah!" François darted forward. "*La voilà!* What did I say?" He clasped the box to his breast. "What did I say?"

"But it is not so!" cried Jacques. "What did you say? You said you had not seen the box! What did *I* say? I said—"

"Enough!" commanded Philip. "I will not endure this bickering! Be quiet, François! Little monkey that you are!"

"*M'sieur!*" François was hurt. His sharp little face fell into lines of misery.

"Little monkey," continued Philip inexorably, "with more thought for your chattering than for my welfare."

"Ah no, no, m'sieur! I swear it is not so! By the—"

"I do not want your oaths," said Philip cruelly. "Am I to wait all night for my cravat, while you revile the good Jacques?"

François cast the box from him.

"Ah, *misérable*! The cravat! *Malheureux*, get thee gone!" He waved agitated hands at Jacques. "You hinder me! You retard me! You upset monsieur! *Va-ten!*"

Jacques obeyed meekly, and Philip turned back to the mirror. To him came François, wreathed once more in smiles.

"He means well, *ce bon Jacques*," he said, busy with the cravat. "But he is *sot*, you understand, *très sot!*" He pushed Philip's chin up with a gentle hand. "He annoys m'sieur, *ah oui!* But he is a good *garçon* when all is said."

"It is you who annoy me," answered Philip. "Not so tight, not so tight! Do you wish to choke me?"

"*Pardon*, m'sieur! No, it is not François who annoys you! *Ah, mille fois non!* François—perhaps he is a little monkey, if m'sieur says so, but he is a very good valet, *n'est-ce pas?* A monkey, if m'sieur pleases, but very clever with a cravat. M'sieur has said it himself."

"You are a child," said Philip. "Yes, that is very fair." He studied his reflection. "I am pleased with it."

"Aha!" François clasped his hands delightedly. "M'sieur is no longer enraged! *Voyons*, I go to fetch the vest of m'sieur!"

Presently, kneeling before his master and adjusting his stockings, he volunteered another piece of information.

"Me, I have been in this country before. I understand well the ways of it. I understand the English, oh, *de parte en part!* I know them for a foolish race, *en somme*—saving always m'sieur, who is more French than English—but never, never have I had the misfortune to meet so terrible Englishman as this servant of m'sieur's uncle, this Moggat. *Si entêté, si impoli!* He looks on me with a suspicion! I cannot tell m'sieur of his so churlish demeanour! He thinks, perhaps, that I go to take his fine coat. Bah! I spit upon it! I speak to him as m'sieur has bid me—*très doucement.* He pretends he cannot understand what it is I say! Me, who speak English *aussi bien que le Français!* Deign to enter into these shoes, m'sieur! I tell him I hold him in contempt! He makes a *reniflement* in his nose, and he mutters 'damned leetle frog-eater!' *Grand Dieu*, I could have boxed his ears, the impudent!"

"I hope you did not?" said Philip anxiously.

"Ah, bah! Would I so demean myself, m'sieur? It is I who am of a peaceable nature, *n'est-ce pas?* But Jacques—*voyons, c'est autre chose!* He is possessed of the hot temper, *ce pauvre* Jacques. I fear for that Moggat if he enrages our Jacques." He shook his head solemnly, and picked up the grey satin coat. "If m'sieur would find it convenient to rise? Ah, *bien!*" He coaxed Philip into the coat, bit by bit. "I say to you, m'sieur, I am consumed of an anxiety. Jacques he is a veritable fire-eater when he is roused, not like me, who am always *doux comme un enfant.* I think, perhaps, he will refuse to remain in the house with this pig of a Moggat."

Philip shook out his ruffles.

"I have never noticed that Jacques showed signs of a so violent temper," he remarked.

"But no! Of a surety, he would not exhibit his terrible passion to m'sieur! Is it that I should permit him?"

"Well," Philip slipped a ring on to his finger, "I am sorry for Jacques, but he must be patient. Soon I shall go to a house of my own."

François' face cleared as if by magic.

"M'sieur is kind! A house of his own. *Je me rangerai bien!* M'sieur contemplates a *mariage*, perhaps?"

Philip dropped his snuff-box.

"*Que diable——!*" he began, and checked himself. "Mind your own business, François!"

"*Ah, pardon, m'sieur!*" replied the irrepressible François. "I but thought that m'sieur had the desire to wed, that he should return to England so hurriedly!"

"Hold your tongue!" said Philip sharply. "Understand me, François, I'll have no meddling *bavardage* about me either to my face or below stairs! *C'est entendu?*"

"But yes, m'sieur," said François abashed. "It is that my tongue runs away with me."

"You'd best keep a guard over it," answered Philip curtly.

"Yes, m'sieur!" Meekly he handed Philip his cane and handkerchief. Then, as his master still frowned, "M'sieur is still enraged?" he ventured.

Philip glanced down at him. At the sight of François' anxious, naïve expression, the frown faded, and he laughed.

"You are quite ridiculous," he said.

François broke into responsive smiles at once.

But when Philip had rustled away to join his uncle, the little valet nodded shrewdly to himself and clicked his tongue against the roof of his mouth.

"*En verité, c'est une femme,*" he remarked. "*C'est ce que j'ai cru.*"

111

CHAPTER XII

Philip Plays a Dangerous Game

François endured the detestable Moggat for a week. He was then rewarded for his patience by the news that Philip was shortly to move into a small house in Curzon Street, which belonged to a friend of Tom. This gentleman consented to let his house for the space of two months, as he was going abroad for that time. Philip went to inspect the prospective abode, and found it to be furnished in excellent style. He closed with its owner and went back to Half-Moon Street to break the joyful news to François. From that moment the excitable valet's spirits soared high. He would manage the affairs of the house for m'sieur; he would find m'sieur a *chef*. Philip was content to waive responsibility. François sallied forth with the air of one about to conquer, to find, so he told Philip, the son of his aunt, a very fair *chef* and a good *garçon*. Philip had no idea that François possessed any relations, much less one in London. When he said this, François looked very waggish, and admitted that he himself had forgotten the existence of this cousin until the moment when m'sieur told him of the new home.

"Then, *subitement*, I remember, for m'sieur will require a *chef*, is it not so?"

"Assuredly," said Philip. "But your cousin may not

wish to take service with me, in which case I shall seek an English cook."

"An English cook? Ah, bah! Is it that I would permit m'sieur to be so ill served? No! M'sieur shall have a French *chef, bien sûr*. What does an Englishman know of the *cuisine*? Is m'sieur to be insulted by the tasteless watery vegetables of such as the wife of Moggat? No! I go to find my cousin!"

"Very well," said Philip.

"And then we have a household *bien tenu*. It is our poor Jacques who could not support an Englishman in the house."

"I hope I am not to be excluded?" smiled Philip.

"*M'sieur se moque de moi!* Is it that m'sieur is English? M'sieur is *tout comme un Français*." He bustled away, full of importance.

The cousin was forthcoming, a stout, good-tempered soul, who rejoiced in the name of Marie-Guillaume. François exhibited him with pride, and he was engaged. That ended all Philip's responsibility. François gathered up the reins of government, and in a week they were installed in Curzon Street. Philip had done no more than say that he wished to enter his new abode on Thursday. On Thursday he went out to Ranelagh; when he returned to Half-Moon Street he found that his baggage had gone. He took his leave of Tom, and walked up the road and round the corner, into Curzon Street. His house was as neat as a new pin; his baggage was unpacked; François was complacent. They might have lived in the house for months; there was no disorder, no fuss, none of the slow settling down. François, Jacques, and Marie-Guillaume had fitted into their respective niches in one short hour. Philip was moved to inform François that he was a treasure.

114

That evening he went to a ball given by the Duchess of Queensberry. And there he met Cleone, for the first time since his return to England.

The Duchess welcomed him effusively, for already Philip was a *persona grata* in Society, and much sought after by hostesses. Tom had lost no time in introducing him to the Fashionable World. The ladies were captivated by his French air, and ogled him shamelessly. Then men found that he was, for all his graces, singularly modest and unaffected at heart, and they extended the hand of friendship towards him. People began to look for him, and to be disappointed if he were absent.

Until now, however, Philip had seen nothing of Cleone, but on all sides he had heard of her. She was, he learnt, London's newest beauty.

She was dancing when Philip saw her first, smiling up at her partner with blue eyes that seemed bluer than ever, and lips that lay in a happy curve. Her golden hair was unpowdered and piled in curls upon the top of her head. Philip thought she was more beautiful than ever.

He had stood apart, watching her. She had not seen him; she was not even thinking of him; those eyes were clear and joyous. Who was her partner? Brainless-looking fool! Simpering ninny! Ay, that was all she cared for! Philip's hand clenched slowly on his snuff-box.

"Aha, Jettan! You have espied the lovely Cleone?"

Philip turned. Lord Charles Fairfax stood at his elbow.

"Yes," he said.

"But how stern and forbidding!" exclaimed Fairfax. "What ails you?"

Philip's mouth had lost its hard line.

"I am struck dumb," he answered gaily. "Can you wonder at it?"

"So are we all. She is very beautiful, is she not?"

"Ravishing!" agreed Philip. He saw Cleone's partner lead her to a chair. "Will you present me?"

"What! And destroy my own chances? We have heard of your killing ways with the fair sex!"

"I protest I have been maligned!" cried Philip. "I do implore your mercy! Present me!"

"Against my will, then!" said his lordship roguishly. He walked forward to where Cleone sat.

"Mistress Cleone, have you no smile for the humblest of your admirers?"

Cleone turned her head.

"Oh, Lord Charles! Give you good even, sir! Do you know you have not been near me the whole evening? I am monstrous hurt, I assure you!"

"Dear lady, how was I to come near you?" protested Fairfax. "Until this moment you have been surrounded."

Cleone gave a happy little laugh.

"I am sure 'tis untrue, sir! You delight in teasing me!" Her eyes wandered past him to Philip.

Fairfax drew him forward.

"Mistress Cleone, may I present one who is newly come from Paris, and is, he swears, struck dumb by your beauty? Mr. Jettan, of whom we all know some naughty tales!"

The colour drained from Cleone's cheeks. She felt faint all at once, and her fingers gripped together over her fan. For one moment she thought she must be mistaken. This was not Philip, this foppish gentleman who stood bowing so profoundly! Heavens, he was speaking! It *was* Philip! How could she mistake that square chin?

"Mademoiselle, this is a scarce-hoped-for honour," he said. "I have watched and I have hungered. Lord Charles took pity on me, for which I shall never cease to thank him."

Cleone tried to answer, and failed. Dazedly she stared at him, from the powdered curls of his wig to the diamond buckles on his shoes. Philip! *Philip!* Philip in stiff silks and laces! Philip patched and painted! Philip with jewels scattered about his person, and polished nails! Was she dreaming? This foppish gentleman her blunt Philip? It was incredible, impossible! What was he saying now?

"I little thought to find you here, mademoiselle! You are with Madame Charteris, no doubt?"

Cleone collected her scattered wits. An awful numbness was stealing over her.

"No, I—I am with my aunt, Lady Malmerstoke," she answered.

"Lady Malmerstoke . . . ?" Philip raised his quizzing-glass with one delicate white hand, and through it scanned the room. "Ah yes, the lady in the apple-green toilette! I remember her well, that lady."

"Oh—do you—do you know her?" asked Cleone. She could not drag her eyes from his face.

"I had the felicity of meeting her some nights ago. I forget where."

"R—really!" Cleone decided that this was a nightmare.

Philip sat down beside her.

"You have been long in town, mademoiselle? You find all this very fatiguing, no doubt?" He waved a languid hand.

117

Indignation was dispersing the numbness. How dared Philip drawl at her like this? How dared he behave as though they were strangers?

"I have been in London nigh on a month. I do not find it fatiguing at all. I enjoy it."

Slowly the straight brows rose.

"But how refreshing!" said Philip. "When everyone is *ennuyé à l'agonie*, how delightful to meet one who frankly enjoys." He looked at her admiringly. "And enjoyment becomes you better than boredom becomes other women."

Cleone felt that she was drifting further and further into the nightmare.

"I am happy to find favour in your eyes, sir. When did you return from Paris?"

"A fortnight since. In a fog which chilled me to the marrow. Almost I fled back to France. But now"—he bowed gracefully—"I thank a kindly Fate which forbade me to retreat thus precipitately."

"Indeed?" said Cleone tartly. "How do you find Sir Maurice?"

"As yet I have not found him," replied Philip. There was a laugh at the back of his eyes. How dared he laugh at her? "I have written to beg him to honour my house with his presence."

"You do not propose to go to him?" Cleone's voice trembled.

Philip started.

"Mademoiselle speaks *en plaisantant*? The country in this weather?" He shuddered.

"I see," said Cleone, and thought that she spoke the truth. Her foot tapped the ground angrily. Philip eyed it through his glass.

"That little foot . . ." he said softly. It was withdrawn. "Ah, cruel! It inspired me with—I think—a madrigal. Cased in silver satin . . . Ah!"

"It pleases you to make merry of my foot, sir?"

"Jamais de ma vie!" Philip threw out his hands. "It is neither food for merriment nor sighs. It is food for pure joy. My eye, *chère mademoiselle,* is susceptible to beauty, be it beauty of face, or beauty of foot; the eye whispers to the brain, and a madrigal blossoms. I dare swear you have listened to an hundred such? Everywhere I have heard tell of your conquests until I am nigh dead with jealousy."

"How very absurd!" tittered Cleone.

"Absurd? Ah, if I could think that!"

"I do not understand you, sir!"

"I can only beg that I, too, may worship at those little feet."

"Mr. Jettan, I can only beg that you will cease to make yourself ridiculous."

"If it is ridiculous to adore, then must I refuse to obey you, fairest. For the sake of one smile, all would I do, save that which is without my power."

Cleone's eyes glittered.

"You have become very adept at flattery, sir."

"But no! Flattery shall never be among my accomplishments, even were it necessary, which here"—he smiled ardently—"it most assuredly is not."

"You surprise me, sir! I thought Paris to be the home of flattery."

"On l'a diffamée. Paris teaches appreciation."

"La!" Cleone, too, could be affected. "You go too deep for me, Mr. Jettan! I fear I am no match for your wit. I am but newly come from the country." The words bit.

"It is almost inconceivable," he said, studying her with the air of a connoisseur.

"Almost as inconceivable as the fact that little more than six months ago you despised all this!" She made a gesture with her fan towards his shimmering coat.

"Was it only six months? It seems to belong to another life. You remember so well, mademoiselle."

"I?" Cleone saw her mistake, and made haste to cover it. "No, sir. It is dear Sir Maurice who remembers." Her eyes sought his face for some change of expression. But not an eyelash flickered; Mr. Jettan was still smiling.

"Now I am desolated!" he sighed. "Mademoiselle Cleone does not remember the manner of my going? But I see that it is so. She is blessed with forgetfulness."

Cleone's heart leapt. Was there a note of *pique*, of hurt, in the smooth voice.

"My memory is not of the longest either, mademoiselle, but I am sure that I am indebted to you."

"Really? I think you must be mistaken, sir."

"It is possible," he bowed. "Yet I seem to recollect that 'twas you who bade me go—to learn to be a gentleman."

Cleone laughed carelessly.

"Did I?—It is so long ago, I have forgotten. And—and here is Mr. Winton come to claim me!"

Philip glanced round quickly. Young James Winton was threading his way towards them. Philip sprang up.

"James!" He held out his hands to the puzzled youth. "You have forgotten, James? And it is, so mademoiselle tells me, but six months since I saw you every day."

Winton stared. Then suddenly he grasped Philip's jewelled hand.

"Jettan—Philip! Merciful heavens, man, is it indeed you?"

"He is quite transformed, is he not?" said Cleone lightly. A little barb was piercing her heart that Philip should show such pleasure at seeing James, and merely bored affectation with her.

Philip's gay laugh rang out.

"I shall write a sonnet in melancholy vein," he promised. "A sonnet to 'Friends Who Knew Me Not'. It will be a *chef-d'œuvre*, and I shall send it to you tied with a sprig of myrtle."

Winton stepped back the better to observe him.

"Thunder and turf, 'tis marvellous! What's this about a sonnet? Don't tell me ye have turned poet!"

"In Paris they do not love my verses," mourned Philip. "They would say, 'No *le petit Philippe se trompe.*' But you shall see! Where are you staying?"

"With Darchit—in Jermyn Street. I came to London in my lady's train." He bowed to Cleone.

Philip's eyes narrowed.

"Aha! James, you will come to a card-party that I am giving to-morrow? I am at 14 Curzon Street."

"Thank you very much, I shall be delighted. Have you set up a house of your own?"

"Sir Humphrey Grandcourt has hired his house to me for a month or so. My *ménage* will amuse you. I am ruled by my valet, the redoubtable François."

"A French valet!"

"But yes! He would allow no English servant to insult me with his boorishness, so I have his cousin for *chef*." He threw a laughing glance at Cleone. "You would smile, mademoiselle, could you but hear his so fierce denunciation of the English race."

Cleone forced a laugh.

"I suppose he does not regard you as English, Mr. Jettan?"

"If I suggest such a thing he accuses me of mocking

121

him. Ah, there is Miss Florence who beckons me! Mademoiselle will excuse me?" He bowed with a great flourish. "I shall hope to be allowed to wait on Madame, your aunt. James, do not forget! To-morrow at 14 Curzon Street!" He swept round on his heel and went quickly to where Mistress Florence Farmer was seated. Cleone watched him kiss the lady's plump hand, and saw the ogling glances that Florence sent him. Desperately she sought to swallow the lump in her throat. She started to flirt with the adoring James. Out of the corner of his eye Philip watched her.

Scalding tears dropped on to Cleone's pillow that night. Philip had returned, indifferent, *blasé*, even scornful! Philip who had once loved her so dearly, Philip who had once been so strong and masterful, was now a dainty, affected Court gallant. Why, why had she sent him away? And, oh, how dared he treat her with that mocking admiration? Suddenly Cleone sat up.

"I hate him!" she told the bed-post. "I hate him, and hate him, and hate him."

Philip was smiling when François disrobed him, a smile that held much of tenderness.

"*Cela marche,*" decided François. "I go to have a mistress."

CHAPTER XIII

Sir Maurice Comes to Town

A tall gentleman rang the bell of Mr. Thomas Jettan's house with some vigour. The door was presently opened by the depressed Moggat.

"Where's your master, Moggat?" demanded the visitor abruptly.

Moggat held the door wide.

"In the library, sir. Will you step inside?"

Sir Maurice swept in. He gave his cloak and hat to Moggat and walked to the library door. Moggat watched him somewhat fearfully. It was not often that Sir Maurice showed signs of perturbation.

"By the way—" Sir Maurice paused, looking back. "My baggage follows me."

"Very good, sir."

Sir Maurice opened the door and disappeared.

Thomas was seated at his desk, but at the sound of the opening door he turned.

"Why, Maurry!" He sprang up. "Gad, this is a surprise! How are ye, lad?" He wrung his brother's hand.

Sir Maurice flung a sheet of paper on to the table.

"What the devil's the meaning of *that*?" he demanded.

"Why the heat?" asked the surprised Thomas.

123

"Read that—that impertinence!" ordered Sir Maurice.

Tom picked up the paper and spread it open. At sight of the writing he smiled.

"Oh, Philip!" he remarked.

"Philip? Philip write me that letter? It's no more Philip than—than a cock-robin!"

Tom sat down.

"Oh, yes it is!" he said. "I recognise his hand. Now don't tramp up and down like that, Maurry! Sit down!" He glanced down the sheet and smothered a laugh.

"'My, very dear Papa,' he read aloud. 'I do trust that you are enjoying your Customary Good Health and that these fogs and bitter winds have not permeated so far as to Little Fittledean. As you will observe by the above written address, I have returned to this most barbarous land. For how long I shall allow myself to be persuaded to remain I cannot tell you, but after the affinity of Paris and the charm of the Parisians, London is quite insupportable. But for the present I remain, *malgré tout*. You will forgive me, I know, that I do not come to visit you at the Pride. The mere thought of the country at this season fills me with incalculable dismay. So I suggest, dear Father, that you honour me by enlivening with your presence this house that I have acquired from Sir Humphrey Grandcourt. Some small entertainment I can promise you, and my friends assure me that the culinary efforts of my *chef* are beyond compare. An exaggeration, believe me, which one who has tasted the wonders of a Paris *cuisine* will easily descry. I have to convey to you the compliments of M. de Château-Banvau and others. I would write more but that I am in labour with an ode. Believe me, Dear Fa-

ther, thy most devoted, humble, and obedient son,—
PHILIPPE.'" Tom folded the paper. "Very proper,"
he remarked. "What's amiss?"

Sir Maurice had stalked to the window. Now he
turned.

"What's amiss? Everything's amiss! That Philip—my
son Philip!—should write me a—an impertinent letter
like that! It's—it's monstrous!"

"For God's sake, sit down, Maurry! You're as bad as
Philip himself for restlessness! Now I take this as a
very dutiful, filial letter."

"Dutiful be damned!" snorted Sir Maurice. "Has
the boy no other feelings than he shows in that letter?
Why did he not come down to see me?"

Tom re-opened the letter.

"The mere thought of the country at this season ap-
palled him. What's wrong with that? You have said
the same."

"I? I? What matters it what I should have said? I
thought Philip cared for me! He trusts I will enliven
his house with my presence! I'm more like to break
my stick across his back!"

"Not a whit," said Tom, cheerfully. "You sent Philip
away to acquire polish, and I don't know what besides. He has obeyed you. Is it likely that, being what
he now is, he'll fly back to the country? What's the
matter with you, Maurice? Are you grumbling because he has obeyed your behests?"

Sir Maurice sank on to the couch.

"If you but knew how I have missed him and
longed for him," he began, and checked himself. "I
am well served," he said bitterly. "I should have been
content to have him as he was."

"So I thought at the time, but I've changed my
opinion."

"I cannot bear to think of Philip as being callous, flippant, and—a mere fop!"

"'Twould be your own fault if he were," said Tom severely. "But he's not. Something inside him has blossomed forth. Philip is now pure joy."

Sir Maurice grunted.

"It's true, lad. That letter—oh, ay! He's a young rascal, but 'twas to avenge his injured feelings, I take it. He was devilish hurt when you and Cleone sent him away betwixt you. He's still hurt that you should have done it. I can't fathom the workings of his mind, but he assures me they are very complex. He is glad that you sent him, but he wants you to be sorry. Or rather, Cleone. The lad is very forgiving to you"—Tom laughed—"but that letter is a spice of devilry—he has plenty of it, I warn you! He hoped you'd be as angry as you are and wish your work undone. There's no lack of affection."

Sir Maurice looked up.

"He's—the same Philip?"

"Never think it! In a way he's the same, but there's more of him—ay, and a score of affectations. In about ten minutes"—he glanced at the clock—"he'll be here. So you'll see for yourself."

Sir Maurice straightened himself. He sighed.

"An old fool, eh, Tom? But it cut me to the quick, that letter."

"Of course it did, the young devil! Oh, Maurry, Maurry, ye never saw the like of our Philip!"

"Is he so remarkable? I heard about that absurd duel, as I told you. There'll be a reckoning between him and Cleone."

"Ay. That's what I don't understand. The pair of them are playing a queer game. Old Sally Malmerstoke told me that Cleone vows she hates Philip. The

126

chit is flirting outrageously with every man who comes—always under Philip's nose. And Philip laughs. Yet I'll swear he means to have her. I don't interfere. They must work out their own quarrel."

"Clo doesn't hate Philip," said Sir Maurice. "She was pining for him until that fool Bancroft read us Satterthwaite's letter. Was it true that Philip fought over some French hussy?"

"No, over Clo herself. But he says naught, and if the truth were told, I believe it's because he has had *affaires* in Paris, even if that was not one. He's too dangerously popular."

"So it seemed from Satterthwaite's account. Is he so popular? I cannot understand it."

"He's novel, y'see. I'd a letter from Château-Banvau the other day, mourning the loss of *ce cher petit Philippe,* and demanding whether he had found his heart or no!"

Sir Maurice drove his cane downwards.

"By Gad, if Philip's so great a success, it's—it's more than ever I expected," he ended lamely.

"Wait till you see him!" smiled Thomas. "The boy's for all the world like a bit o' quicksilver. He splutters out French almost every time he opens his mouth, and—here he is!"

A door banged loudly outside, and a clear, crisp voice floated into the library from the hall.

"*Mordieu,* what a climate! Moggat, you rogue, am I not depressed enough without your glum face to make me more so? Smile, *vieux cérpin,* for the love of God!"

"Were I to call Moggat one-half of the names Philip bestows on him, he'd leave me," remarked Tom. "With him, Philip can do no wrong. Now what's to do?"

"*Doucement, malheureux!* Gently, I say! Do you

wish to pull my arms off with the coat? *Ah, voilà!*
Spread it to dry, Moggat, and take care not to crease
it. Yes, that is well!"

Then came Moggat's voice, very self-conscious.

"*C'est comme moosoo désire?*"

There was a sound of hand-clapping, and an
amused laugh.

"*Voyons, c'est fameux!* Quite the French scholar,
eh, Moggat? Where's my uncle? In the library?"

Came a quick step across the hall. Philip swirled
into the room.

"Much have I borne in silence, Tom, but this
rain—" He broke off. The next moment he was on
one knee before his father, Sir Maurice's thin hands
pressed to his lips. "Father!"

Tom coughed and walked to the window.

Sir Maurice drew his hands away. He took Philip's
chin in his long fingers and forced his head up. Si-
lently he scrutinised his son's face. Then he smiled.

"You patched and painted puppy-dog," he mimicked softly.

Philip laughed. His hands found Sir Maurice's
again and gripped hard.

"Alack, too true! Father, you're looking older."

"Impudent young scapegrace! What would you? I
have but one son."

"And you missed him?"

"A little," acknowledged Sir Maurice.

Philip rose to his feet.

"Ah, but I am glad! And you are sorry you sent him
away?"

"Not now. But when I received this—very." Sir
Maurice held out the sheet of paper.

"That! Bah!" Philip sent it whirling into the fire.
"For that I apologise. If you had not been hurt—oh,
128

heaven knows what I should have done! Where is your baggage, Father?"

"Here by now."

"Here? But no, no! It must go to Curzon Street!"

"My dear son, I thank you very much, but an old man is better with an old man."

Tom wheeled round.

"What's that? Who are you calling an old man, Maurry? I'm as young as ever I was!"

"In any case, it is to Curzon Street that you come, Father."

"As often as you wish, dear boy, but I'll stay with Tom." Then, as Philip prepared to argue the point, "No, Philip, my mind is made up. Sit down and tell me the tale of your ridiculous duel with Bancroft."

"Oh, that!" Philip laughed. "It was amusing, but scandalous. My sympathies were with my adversary."

"And what was the ode you threatened to read?"

"An ode to importunate friends, especially composed for the occasion. They took it from me—Paul and Louis—oh, and Henri de Chatelin! They do not like my verse."

Sir Maurice lay back in his seat and laughed till the tears ran down his cheeks.

"Gad, Philip, but I wish I'd been there! To hear you declaim an ode of your own making! Faith, is it really my blunt, brusque, impossible Philip?"

"Not at all! It is your elegant, smooth, and wholly possible Philip!"

Sir Maurice sat up again.

"Ah! And does this Philip contemplate marriage?"

"That," said his son, "is on the knees of the gods."

"I see. Is it woe unto him who seeks to interfere?"

"*Parfaitement!*" bowed Philip. "I play now—a little game."

"And Cleone?"

"Cleone . . . I don't know. It is what I wish to find out. Lady Malmerstoke stands my friend."

"Trust Sally," said Tom.

Philip's eyes sparkled.

"Ah, Tom, Tom, art a rogue! Father, he is in love with her ladyship!"

"He always has been," answered Sir Maurice. "Even before old Malmerstoke died."

Tom cleared his throat.

"I—"

"Then why do you not wed her?" demanded Philip.

"She will not. Now she says—perhaps. We are very good friends," he added contentedly. "I doubt neither of us is at the age when one loves with heat."

"Philip, how do you like Paris?" interrupted Sir Maurice.

"I cannot tell you, sir! My feeling for Paris and my Paris friends is beyond all words."

"Ay. I thought the same. But in the end one is glad to come home."

"May it please heaven, then, to make the end far, far away," said Philip. "When I go back, you will go with me, Father."

"Ah, I am too old for that now," answered Sir Maurice. He smiled reminiscently.

"Too old? *Quelle absurdité!*" M. de Château-Banvau has made me swear to bring you. M. de Richelieu asked when he was to see your face again. A score—"

"De Richelieu? Where did you meet him, boy?"

"At Versailles. He was very kind to me for your sake."

"Ay, he would be. So you went to Versailles, then!"

"Often."

"Philip, I begin to think you are somewhat of a rake. What attracted you to Versailles?"

"Many things," parried Philip.

"Female things?"

"What curiosity! Sometimes, yes, but not *au sérieux.*'

"Little Philip without a heart, eh?"

"Who told you that?" Philip leaned forward.

"Satterthwaite wrote it, or something like it."

"*Le petit Phillipe au Coeur Perdu.* Most of them would give their eyes to know who the fair unknown may be!"

"Is it still Cleone?" Sir Maurice looked sharply across at him.

"It has—never been anyone else," answered Philip simply.

"I am glad. I want you to marry her, Philip."

"Sir," said Philip superbly, "I have every intention of so doing."

CHAPTER XIV

The Strange Behavior of Mistress Cleone

"François, there is one below who desires m'sieu'."

François shook out a fine lace ruffle.

"*Qui est-ce?*"

"*Le père de m'sieur,*" answered Jacques gloomily.

François cast the ruffle aside.

"*Le père de m'sieur!* I go at once." He vanished out of the door and scuttled downstairs to the library. Sir Maurice was startled by his sudden entrance, and raised his eyeglass the better to observe this very abrupt, diminutive creature.

François bowed very low.

"M'sieu', eet ees zat my mastaire 'e ees wiz hees *barbier*. Eef m'sieu' would come up to ze chamber of my mastaire?"

Sir Maurice smiled.

"*Assurément. Vous allez marcher en tête?*"

François' face broke into a delighted smile.

"*Ah, m'sieur parle Français! Si m'sieur veut me suivre?*"

"*M'sieur veut bien,*" nodded Sir Maurice. He followed François upstairs to Philip's luxurious bedroom. François put forward a chair.

"M'sieur will be graciously pleased to seat himself? M'sieur Philippe will come very soon. It is the visit of the barber, you understand."

"A serious matter," agreed Sir Maurice.

"M'sieur understands well. Me. I am valet of M'sieur Philippe."

"I had guessed it. You are François?"

"Yes, m'sieur. It is perhaps that M'sieur Philippe has spoken of me?" He looked anxiously at Sir Maurice.

"Certainly he has spoken of you," smiled Sir Maurice.

"It is perhaps—that he tell you I am *un petit singe?*"

"No, he said no such thing," answered Sir Maurice gravely. "He told me he possessed a veritable treasure for valet."

"Ah!" François clapped his hands. "It is true, m'sieur. I am a very good valet—oh, but very good!" He skipped to the bed and picked up an embroidered satin vest. This he laid over a chairback.

"The vest of M'sieur Philippe," he said reverently.

"So I see," said Sir Maurice. "What's he doing, lying abed so late?"

"Ah, non, m'sieur! He does not lie abed late! Oh, but never, never. It is that the barber is here, and the tailor—imbeciles, both! They put M'sieur Philippe in a bad humour with their so terrible stupidity. He spends an hour explaining what it is that he wishes." François cast up his eyes. "And they do not understand, no! They are of so great a density! M'sieur Philippe he become much enraged, naturally."

"Monsieur Philippe is very particular, eh?"

François beamed. He was opening various pots in readiness for his master.

"Yes, m'sieur. M'sieur Philippe must have everything just as he likes it."

At that moment Philip walked in, wrapped in a

134

gorgeous silk robe, and looking thunderous. When he saw his father his brow cleared.

"You, sir? Have you waited long?"

"No, only ten minutes or so. Have you strangled the tailor?"

Philip laughed.

"*De près!* François, I will be alone with m'sieur."

François bowed. He went out with his usual hurried gait.

Philip sat down before his dressing-table.

"What do you think of the incomparable François?" he asked.

"He startled me at first," smiled Sir Maurice. "A droll little creature."

"But quite inimitable. You're out early this morning, sir?"

"My dear Philip, it is close on noon! I have been to see Cleone."

Philip picked up a nail-polisher and passed it gently across his fingers.

"Ah?"

"Philip, I am worried."

"Yes?" Philip was intent on his nails. "And why?"

"I don't understand the child! I could have sworn she was dying for you to return!"

Philip glanced up quickly.

"That is true?"

"I thought so. At home—yes, I am certain of it! But now she seems a changed being." He frowned, looking at his son. Philip was again occupied with his hands. "She is in excellent spirits; she tells me that she enjoys every moment of every day. While I was there three posies arrived from admirers. She was in ecstasies! I spoke of you and she was quite indifferent. What have you done to make her so, Philip?"

"I do not quite know. I have become what she would have had me. To test her, I aped the mincing extravagance of the typical town-gallant. She was surprised at first, and then angry. That pleased me. I thought: Cleone does not like the thing I am; she would prefer the real me. Then I waited on Lady Malmerstoke. Cleone was there. She was, as you say, quite changed. I suppose she was charming; it did not seem so to me. She laughed and flirted with her fan; she encouraged me to praise her beauty; she demanded the madrigal I had promised her. When I read it she was delighted. She asked her aunt if I were not a dreadful, flattering creature. Then came young Winton, who is, I take it, *amoureux à en perdre la tête*. To him she was all smiles, behaving like some Court miss. Since then she has always been the same. She is kind to every man who comes her way and to me. You say you do not understand? Nor do I. She is not the Cleone I knew, and not the Cleone I love. She makes herself as—Clothilde de Chaucheron. *Charmante, spirituelle*, one to whom a man makes trifling love, but not the one a man will wed." He spoke quietly, and with none of his usual sparkle.

Sir Maurice leaned forward, striking his fist on his knee.

"But she is not that type of woman, Philip! That's what I can't understand!"

Philip shrugged slightly.

"She is not, you say? I wonder now whether that is so. She flirted before, you remember, with Bancroft."

"Ay! To tease you!"

"*Cela se peut*. This time it is not to tease me. That I know."

"But, Philip, if it is not for that, why does she do it?"

"Presumably because she so wishes. It is possible that the adulation she receives has flown to her head. It is almost as though she sought to captivate me."

"Cleone would never do such a thing!"

"Well, sir, you will see. Come with us this afternoon. Tom and I are bidden to take a dish of Bohea with her ladyship."

"Sally has already asked me. I shall certainly come. *Mordieu*, what ails the child?"

Philip rubbed some rouge on to his cheeks.

"If you can tell me the answer to that riddle, sir, I shall—thank you."

"You do care, Philip? Still?" He watched Philip pick up the haresfoot with fingers that trembled a little.

"Care?" said Philip. "I—yes, sir. I care—greatly."

*   *   *

Lady Malmerstoke glanced critically at her niece.

"You are very gay, Clo," she remarked.

"Gay?" cried Cleone. "How could I be sober, Aunt Sally? I am enjoying myself so much!"

Lady Malmerstoke pushed a bracelet farther up one plump arm.

"H'm!" she said. "It's very unfashionable, my dear, not to say *bourgeois*."

"Oh, fiddle!" answered Cleone. "Who thinks that?"

"I really don't know. It is what one says. To be in the mode you must be fatigued to death."

"Then I am not in the mode," laughed Cleone. "Don't forget, Aunt, that I am but a simple country-maid!" She swept a mock curtsy.

"No," said her ladyship placidly. "One is not like to forget it."

"What do you mean?" demanded Cleone.

"Don't eat me," sighed her aunt. "'Tis your principal charm—freshness."

"Oh!" said Cleone doubtfully.

"Or it was," added Lady Malmerstoke, folding her hands and closing her eyes.

"Was! Aunt Sally, I insist that you tell me what it is you mean!"

"My love, you know very well what I mean."

"No, I do not! I—I—Aunt Sally, wake up!"

Her ladyship's brown eyes opened.

"Well, my dear, if you must have it, 'tis this—you make yourself cheap by your flirtatious ways."

Cleone's cheeks flamed.

"I—oh, I don't f—flirt! I—Auntie, how can you say so?"

"Quite easily," said her ladyship. "Else had I left it unsaid. Since this Mr. Philip Jettan has returned you have acquired all the tricks of the sex. I do not find it becoming in you, but mayhap I am wrong."

"It has nothing to do with Ph—Mr. Jettan!"

"I beg your pardon, my dear, I thought it had. But if you wish to attract him—"

"Aunt!" almost shrieked Cleone.

"I wish you would not interrupt," complained Lady Malmerstoke wearily. "I said if you wish to attract him you should employ less obvious methods."

"H—how *dare* you, Aunt Sally! I wish to attract him? I hate him! I hate the very sight of him!"

The sleepy brown eyes grew more alert.

"Is that the way the wind lies?" murmured Lady Malmerstoke. "What's he done?" she added, ever practical.

"He hasn't done anything. He—I—"

"Then what hasn't he done?"

138

"Aunt Sally—Aunt Sally—you—I won't answer! He —nothing at all! 'Tis merely that I do not like him."

"It's not apparent in your manner," remarked her ladyship. "Are you determined that he shall fall in love with you?"

"Of course I never thought of such a thing! I—why should I?"

"For the pleasure of seeing him at your feet, and then kicking him away. Revenge, my love, revenge."

"How dare you say such things, Aunt! It—it isn't true!"

Lady Malmerstoke continued to pursue her own line of thought.

"From all I can see of this Philip, he's not the man to be beaten by a chit of a girl. I think he is in love with you. Have a care, my dear. Men with chins like his are not safe. I've had experience, and I know. He'll win in the end, if he has a mind to do so."

"Mind!" Cleone was scornful. "He has no mind above clothes or poems!"

Lady Malmerstoke eyed her lazily.

"Who told you that, Clo?"

"No one. I can see for myself!"

"There's nothing blinder than a very young woman," philosophised her ladyship. "One lives and one learns. Your Philip—"

"He isn't my Philip!" cried Cleone, nearly in tears.

"You put me out," complained her aunt. "Your Philip is no fool. He's dangerous. On account of that chin, you understand. Don't have him, my dear; he's one of your masterful men. They are the worst; old Jeremy Fletcher was like that. Dear me, what years ago that was!"

"He—he's no more masterful than—than his uncle!"

"No, thank heaven, Tom's an easy-going creature," agreed her aunt. "A pity Philip is not the same."

"But I tell you he is! If—if he were more masterful I should like him better! I like a man to be a man and not—a—a pranked-out doll!"

"How you have changed!" sighed her aunt. "I thought that was just what you did not want. Didn't you send your Philip away to become a beau?"

"He is not my Philip—Aunt! I—no, of course I did—didn't. And if I d-did, it was very st-stupid of me, and now I'd rather have a—a masterful man."

"Ay, we're all like that in our youth," nodded her aunt. "When you grow older you'll appreciate the milder sort. I nearly married Jerry Fletcher. Luckily I changed my mind and had Malmerstoke. God rest his soul, poor fellow! Now I shall have Tom, I suppose."

Cleone broke into a hysterical laugh.

"Aunt, you are incorrigible! How can you talk so?"

"Dreadful, isn't it? But I was always like that. Very attractive, you know. I never was beautiful, but I made a great success. I quite shocked my poor mother. But it was all a pose, of course. It made me noticed. I was so amusing and novel—like you, my love, but in a different way. All a pose."

"Why, is it still a pose, Aunt?"

"Oh, now it's a habit. So much less fatiguing, my dear. But to return to what I was saying, you—"

"Don't—don't let's talk—about me," begged Cleone unsteadily. "I—hardly know what possesses me, but—Oh, there's the bell!"

Lady Malmerstoke dragged herself up.

"Already? Clo, is my wig on straight? Drat the men, I've not had a wink of sleep the whole afternoon. A nice hag I shall look to-night. Which of them is it, my dear?"

140

Cleone was peering out of the window.

"'Tis James and Jennifer, Aunt." She came back into the room. "It seems an age since I saw Jenny."

Lady Malmerstoke studied herself in her little mirror.

"Is she the child who lives down in the country?"

"Yes—Jenny Winton, such a sweet little thing. She has come up with Mr. Winton for a few weeks. I am so glad she managed to induce him to bring her!" Cleone ran forward as the two Wintons were ushered in "Jenny, dear!"

Jennifer was half a head shorter than Cleone, a shy child with soft grey eyes and mouse-coloured hair. She flung her arms round Cleone's neck.

"Oh, Clo, how prodigious elegant you look!" she whispered.

"And oh, Jenny, how pretty you look!" retorted Cleone. "Aunt Sally, this is my dear Jennifer!"

Jennifer curtseyed.

"How do you do, ma'am?" she said in a voice fluttering with nervousness.

"I am very well, child. Come and sit down beside me." She patted the couch invitingly. "Is this your first visit to town, my dear?"

Jennifer sat down on the edge of the couch. She stole an awed glance at Lady Malmerstoke's powdered wig.

"Yes, ma'am. It is so exciting."

"I'll warrant it is! And have you been to many balls, yet?"

"N-no." The little face clouded over. "Papa does not go out very much," she explained.

Cleone sank on to a stool beside them, her silks swirling about her.

"Oh, Auntie, please take Jenny to the Dering ball

141

next week!" she said impulsively. "You will come, won't you, sweet?"

Jennifer blushed and stammered.

"To be sure," nodded her ladyship. "Of course she will come! James, sit down! You should know by now how the sight of anyone on their feet fatigues me, silly boy! Dear me, child, how like you are to your brother! Are you looking at my wig? Monstrous, isn't it?"

Jennifer was covered with confusion.

"Oh, no ma'am, I—"

Her ladyship chuckled.

"Of course you were. How could you help it? Cleone tells me it is a ridiculous creation, don't you, my love?"

"I do, and I truly think it!" answered Cleone, her eyes dancing. " 'Tis just a little more impossible than the last."

"There!" Lady Malmerstoke turned back to Jennifer. "She is an impertinent hussy, is she not?"

"Could she be impertinent?" asked James fondly.

"Very easily she could and is," nodded her ladyship. "A minx."

"Oh!" Jennifer was shocked.

"Don't attend to her!" besought Cleone. "Sometimes she is very ill-natured, as you see."

Jennifer ventured a very small laugh. She had resolutely dragged her eyes from the prodigious wig, and was now gazing at Cleone.

"You—you seem quite different," she told her.

Cleone shook her golden head.

" 'Tis only that Aunt Sally has tricked me out in fine clothes," she replied. "I'm—oh, I am the same!" she laughed, but not very steadily. "Am I not, James?"

"Always the same," he said ardently. "Always beautiful."

"I will not have it," said Lady Malmerstoke severely. "You'll turn the child's head, if 'tis not turned already."

"Oh, it is, it is!" cried Cleone. "I am quite too dreadfully vain! And there is the bell again! James, who is it? It's vastly bad-mannered to peep, but you may do it. Quick!"

James went to the window.

"Too late," he said. "They are in, whoever they are."

" 'Twill be Thomas," decided Lady Malmerstoke. "I wonder if he is any fatter?"

Jennifer giggled. She had never met anything quite like this queer, voluminous old lady before.

"Is—is Sir Maurice coming?" she inquired.

"I told him to be sure to come," answered her ladyship. "You know him, don't you?"

"Oh, yes!" breathed Jennifer.

"Sah Maurice and Mr. Jettan," announced the little black page.

"Drat!" said her ladyship. She rose. "Where's your son?" she demanded, shaking her finger at Sir Maurice.

Sir Maurice kissed her hand.

"Sally, you grow ruder and ruder," he reproved her.

"Maurice," she retorted, "you were ever a punctilious ramrod. Philip's the only one of you I want to see. He says such audacious things," she explained. "So gratifying to an old woman. Well, Tom?"

Thomas bowed very low.

"Well, Sally?"

"That's not polite," she said. "You can see I am very well. I declare you are growing thinner!"

Thomas drew himself up sheepishly.

"Am I, my dear?"

Her ladyship gave a little crow of delight.

"You've been taking exercise!" she exclaimed. "If you continue at this rate—I vow I'll marry you in a month!"

"I wish you would, my dear," said Tom seriously.

"Oh, I shall one day, never fear!" She caught sight of Jennifer's astonished expression and chuckled. "Now, Tom, behave yourself! You are shocking the child!" she whispered.

"I? What have I done? She's shocked at your forwardness!"

Sir Maurice had walked over to Cleone. She held out her hands, and he made as if to kiss them. She snatched them back.

"Oh, no, no!" she cried. "Sir Maurice!"

He smiled down at her upturned face.

"In truth, my dear, you've so changed from the little Cleone I know that I dare take no liberties."

Her mouth quivered suddenly; she caught at the lapels of his coat.

"No, no, don't say it, sir! I am the same! Oh, I am, I am!"

"What's Cleone doing?" inquired Lady Malmerstoke. "Kissing Maurice? Now who's forward?"

Cleone smiled through her tears.

"You are, Aunt Sally. And you are in a very teasing humour!"

Sir Maurice pressed her hands gently. He turned to the curtseying Jennifer.

"Why, Jenny? This is a surprise! How are you, child?"

"Very well, I thank you, sir," she answered. "Very happy to be in London."

"The first visit! Where are you staying?"

"With Grandmamma, out at Kensington," she said. Lady Malmerstoke clutched Tom's arm.

"Kensington, poor child!" she murmured. "For heaven's sake everyone sit down! No, Maurice, that chair is too low for me. I'll take the couch." She proceeded to do so. As a matter of course, Tom sat down beside her. The others arranged themselves in two pairs, Sir Maurice leading Jennifer to a chair near the fire, and Cleone going to the window-seat with the admiring James.

Five minutes later the bell rang for the third time, and Jennifer received the worst shock of the afternoon. The page announced Mr. Philip Jettan, and Philip came into the room.

Sir Maurice felt Jennifer's start of surprise, and saw her stare past him as though she saw at least three ghosts.

Philip went to his hostess and dropped on one knee to kiss her hand. He was dressed in puce and old gold. Jennifer thought she had never seen anything so gorgeous, or so astonishing. She did not believe for a moment that it was her old playfellow, Philip.

"Madame, I am late!" said Philip. "I ask a thousand pardons!"

"And you are sure you'll receive them!" chuckled her ladyship. "I'd give them, but that it would fatigue me so. Where's that ode? Don't tell me you've forgotten it!"

"Forgotten it! Never! It is a very beautiful ode, too, in my best style. *Le voici!*" He handed her a rolled parchment sheet, tied with mauve ribbons, and with violets cunningly inserted.

"You delightful boy!" cried her ladyship, inspecting

145

it. "Violets! How did you know they were my favourite flowers?"

"I knew instinctively," answered Philip solemnly.

"Of course you did! But how charming of you! I declare I daren't untie it till the violets are dead. Look, Tom, is it not pretty? And isn't Philip sweet to write me an ode?"

"I am looking," said Tom gloomily. "Ye rascal, how dare you try to steal my lady's heart away from me?"

"I should be more than human an I did not!" replied Philip promptly.

Lady Malmerstoke was showing the dainty roll to Sir Maurice.

"An ode to my wig," she told him. "Written in French."

"An ode to your what?" asked Thomas.

"My wig, Tom, my wig! You were not here when we discussed it. Cleone thought it a prodigious ugly wig, but Philip would have none of it. He said such pretty things about it, and promised me an ode for it! Philip, did I thank you?"

Philip was bowing over Cleone's hand. He turned.

"With your eyes, madame, eloquently! But I need no thanks; it was an honour and a joy."

"Think of that!" nodded my lady, looking from Tom to Sir Maurice. "Philip, come and be presented to Mistress Jennifer. Or do you know her?"

Philip released Cleone's hand, and swung round.

"Jennifer! Of course I know her!" He went across the room. "Why, Jenny, where do you spring from? How are you?"

Jennifer gazed up at him with wide eyes.

"Philip? Is—is it really—you?" she whispered.

"You didn't know me? Jenny, how unkind! Surely I haven't changed as much as that?"

146

"Y-you have," she averred. "More!"

"I have not, I swear I have not! Father, go away! Let me sit here and talk to Jennifer!"

Only too glad to obey, Sir Maurice rose.

"He is very peremptory and autocratic, isn't he, my dear?" he smiled.

Philip sank into the vacated chair.

"I—I feel I ought to call you Mr. Jettan!" said Jennifer.

"Jenny! If you dare to do such a thing I shall—I shall—"

"What will you do?"

"Write a canzonet to your big eyes!" he laughed.

Jennifer blushed, and her lips trembled into a smile.

"Will you really? I should like that, I think, Mr. Jettan."

"It shall be ready by noon to-morrow," said Philip at once, "if you will promise not to misname me!"

"But—"

"Jenny, I vow I have not changed so much! 'Tis only my silly clothes!"

"That's—what Clo said when I told her *she* had changed."

"Oh!" Philip shot a glance towards the unconscious Cleone. "Did she say that?"

"Yes. But I think she has changed, don't you?"

"*De tête en pieds*," said Philip slowly.

"What is that?" Jennifer looked rather alarmed.

Philip turned back to her.

"That is a foolish habit, Jenny. They say I chatter French all day. Which is very affected."

"French? Do you talk French now? How wonderful!" breathed Jennifer. "Say something else! Please!"

"*La lumière de tes beaux yeux me pénètre jusqu'au cœur.*" He bowed, smiling.

"Oh! What does that mean?"

"It wouldn't be good for you to know," answered Philip gravely.

"Oh! but I would like to know, I think," she said naïvely.

"I said that—you have very beautiful eyes."

"Did you? How—how dreadful of you! And you won't forget the—the can—can—what you were going to write for me, will you?"

"The canzonet. No, I think it must be a sonnet. And the flower—alas, your flower is out of season!"

"Is it? What is my flower?"

"A daisy."

She considered this.

"I do not like daisies very much. Haven't I another flower?"

"Yes, a snowdrop."

"Oh, that is pretty!" She clapped her hands. "Is it too late for snowdrops?"

"I defy it to be too late!" said Philip. "You shall have them if I have to fly to the ends of the earth for them!"

Jennifer giggled.

"But you couldn't, could you? Cleone! Cleone!"

Cleone came across the room.

"Yes, Jenny? Has Mr. Jettan been saying dreadfully flattering things to you?"

"N-yes, I think he has! And he says I must still call him Philip. And oh! he is going to write a—a sonnet to my eyes, tied with snowdrops! Mr. J—Philip, what is Cleone's flower?"

Philip had risen. He put a chair forward for Cleone.

148

"Can you ask, Jenny? What but a rose?"

Cleone sat down. Her lips smiled steadily.

"A rose? Surely it's a flaunting flower, sir?"

"Ah, mademoiselle, it must be that you have never seen a rose just bursting from the bud!"

"Oh, la! I am overcome, sir! And I have not yet thanked you for the bouquet you sent me this morning!"

Philip's eyes travelled to the violets at her breast.

"I did not send violets," he said mournfully.

Cleone's eyes flashed.

"No. These"—she touched the flowers caressingly—"I have from Sir Deryk Brenderby."

"He is very fortunate, mademoiselle. Would that I were also!"

"I think you are, sir. Mistress Ann Nutley wore your carnations yesterday the whole evening." Cleone found that she was looking straight into his eyes. Hurriedly she looked away, but a pulse was beating in her throat. For one fleeting instant she had seen the old Philip, grave, honest, a little appealing. If only—if only—"

"Mr. Jett—I mean Philip! Will you teach me to say something in French?"

"Why, of course, _chérie_. What would you say?"

The pulse stopped its excited beating; the blue eyes lost their wistful softness. Cleone turned to James, who stood at her elbow.

CHAPTER XV

Lady Malmerstoke on Husbands

"And he brought it himself, yesterday morning, tied with snowdrops. I don't know how he got them, for they are over, are they not, Clo? But there they were, with the prettiest verse you can imagine. It said my eyes were twin pools of grey! Isn't that beautiful?"

Cleone jerked one shoulder.

"It is not very original," she said.

"Don't you like it?" asked Jennifer reproachfully.

Cleone was ashamed of her flash of ill-humour.

"Yes, dear, of course I do. So Mr. Jettan brought it to you himself, did he?"

"Indeed, yes! And stayed a full hour, talking to papa and to me. What do you think? He has begged me to be sure and dance with him on Wednesday! Is it not kind of him?"

"Very," said Cleone dully.

"I cannot imagine why he should want them," Jennifer prattled on. "Jamie says he is at Mistress Nutley's feet. Is she very lovely, Clo?"

"I don't know. Yes, I suppose she is."

"Philip is teaching me to speak French. It is so droll, and he laughs at my accent. Can you speak French, Clo?"

"A little. No doubt he would laugh at my accent if he ever heard it."

"Oh, I do not think so! He could not, could he? Clo, I asked if he did not think you were very beautiful, and he said—"

"Jenny, you must not ask things like that!"

"He did not mind! Truly, he did not! He just laughed—he is always laughing, Clo!—and said that there was no one who did not think so. Was not that neat?"

"Very," said Cleone.

Jennifer drew nearer.

"Cleone, may I tell you a secret?"

A fierce pain shot through Cleone.

"A secret? What is it?" she asked quickly.

"Why, Clo, how strange you look! 'Tis only that I know James to be in love with—you!"

Cleone sank back. She started to laugh from sheer relief.

"I do not see that it is funny," said Jennifer, hurt.

"No, no, dear! It—it is not that—I mean, of course, of course, I knew that James was—was—fond of me."

"Did you? Oh—oh, are you going to marry him?" Jennifer's voice squeaked with excitement.

"Jenny, you ask such dreadful questions! No, I am not."

"But—but he loves you, Clo! Don't you love him?"

"Not like that. James only thinks he loves me. He's too young. I— Tell me about your dress, dear!"

"For the ball?" Jennifer sat up, nothing loth. "'Tis of white silk—"

"Sir Deryk Brenderby!"

Jennifer started.

"Oh, dear!" she said regretfully.

A tall, loose-limbed man came in.

"Fair Mistress Cleone! I am happy, indeed, to have found you in! I kiss your hands, dear lady!"

Cleone drew them away, smiling.

"Mistress Jennifer Winton, Sir Deryk."

Brenderby seemed to become suddenly aware of Jenny's presence. He bowed. Jennifer curtseyed demurely, and took refuge behind her friend.

Sir Deryk lowered himself into a chair.

"Mistress Cleone, can you guess why I have come?"

"To see me!" said Cleone archly.

"That is the obvious, fair tormentor! Another reason had I."

"The first should be enough, sir," answered Cleone, with downcast eyes.

"And is, Most Beautiful. But the other reason concerns you also."

"La! You intrigue me, sir! Pray, what is it?"

"To beg, on my knees, that you will dance with me on Wednesday!"

"Oh, I don't know!" Cleone shook her head. "I doubt all the dances are gone."

"Ah, no, dearest lady! Not all!"

"Indeed, I think so! I cannot promise anything."

"But you give me hope?"

"I will not take it from you," said Cleone. "Perhaps Jennifer will give you a dance."

Sir Deryk did not look much elated. But he bowed to Jennifer.

"May that happiness be mine, madam?"

"Th-thank you," stammered Jennifer. "If you please!"

Sir Deryk bowed again and straightway forgot her existence.

"You wear my primroses, fairest!" he said to Cleone. "I scarce dared to hope so modest a posy would be so honoured."

Cleone glanced down at the pale yellow blooms.

153

"Oh, are they yours? I had forgot," she said cruelly.

"Ah, Cleone!"

Cleone raised her brows.

"My name, sir?"

"Mistress Cleone," corrected Brenderby, bowing.

Lady Malmerstoke chose that moment at which to billow into the room. She leaned on the arm of one Mr. Jettan.

"Philip, you are a sad fellow! You do not mean one word of what you say! Oh, lud! I have chanced on a reception. Give ye good den, Jenny, my dear. Sir Deryk? Thus early in the morning? I think you know Mr. Jettan?"

The two men bowed.

"I have the pleasure, Lady Malmerstoke," said Brenderby. "I did not see you last night, Jettan? You were not at Gregory's card-party?"

"Last night?—last night? No, I was at White's with my father. Mademoiselle, your very obedient! *Et la petite!*"

"*Bonjour, monsieur!*" ventured Jennifer shyly.

Philip swept her a leg.

"*Mademoiselle a fait des grands progrès,*" he said.

She wrinkled her brow.

"Great—progress?" she hazarded.

"Of course! And how is mademoiselle?"

"Very well, I thank you, sir."

Lady Malmerstoke sank into a large armchair.

"Well, I trust I don't intrude?" she remarked. "Clo, where is my embroidery?" She turned to her guests. "I never set a stitch, of course. It would fatigue me too much. But it looks industrious to have it by me, doesn't it?"

154

Cleone and Brenderby had walked to the table in search of the missing embroidery. Cleone looked over her shoulder.

"You must not believe what she says," she told them. "Aunt Sally embroiders beautifully. She is not nearly as lazy as she would have you think."

"Not lazy, my love—indolent. A much nicer word. Thank you, my dear." She received her stitchery and laid it down. "I will tell you all a secret. Oh, Philip knows! Philip, you need not listen."

Philip was perched on a chair-arm.

"A million thanks, Aunt!"

"That is very unkind of you!" she reproached him. "You tell my secret before ever I have time to say a word!"

"*Eh bien!* You should not have suggested that I did not want to listen to your voice."

"When I am, indeed, your aunt, I shall talk to you very seriously about flattering old women," she said severely.

Cleone clapped her hands.

"Oh, Aunt Sally! You are going to wed Mr. Jettan?"

"One of them," nodded her aunt. "I gather that this one"—she smiled up at Philip—"is going to wed Someone Else. And I do not think I would have him in any case."

"And now who is unkind?" cried Philip. "I've a mind to run away with you as you enter the church!"

Cold fear was stealing through Cleone. Mechanically she congratulated her aunt. Through a haze she heard Brenderby's voice and Jennifer's. So Philip was going to marry Someone Else? No doubt it was Ann Nutley, the designing minx!

When Philip came presently to her side she was gayer than ever, sparkling with merriment, and seemingly without a care in the world. She drew Sir Deryk into the conversation, flirting outrageously. She parried all Philip's sallies and laughed at Sir Deryk's witticisms. Then Philip went to talk to Jennifer. A pair of hungry, angry, jealous, and would-be careless blue eyes followed him and grew almost hard.

When the guests had gone Cleone felt as though her head were full of fire. Her cheeks burnt, her eyes were glittering. Lady Malmerstoke looked at her.

"You are hot, my love. Open the window."

Cleone obeyed, cooling her cheeks against the glass panes.

"How very shy that child is!" remarked my lady.

"Jenny? Yes. Very, is she not?"

"I thought Sir Deryk might have noticed her a little more than he did."

"He had no chance, had he? She was quite monopolised."

Her ladyship cast a shrewd glance towards the back of Cleone's head. She smiled unseen.

"Well, my love, to turn to other matters, which is it to be—Philip or Sir Deryk?"

Cleone started.

"What do you mean, Aunt? Which is it to *be*?"

"Which are you going to smile upon? You have given both a deal of encouragement. I don't count young James, of course. He's a babe."

"Please, please—"

"I don't like Sir Deryk. No, I don't like him at all. He has no true politeness, or he would have talked a little more to me, or to Jenny. Which do you intend to wed, my dear?"

"Neither!"

"My dear Cleone!" Her ladyship was shocked.

"Then why do you encourage them to make love to you? Now be advised by me! Have Sir Deryk!"

Cleone gave a trembling laugh.

"I thought you did not like him?"

"No more I do. But that's not to say he'd make a bad husband. On the contrary. He'd let you do as you please, and he'd not be for ever pestering you with his presence."

"For these very reasons I'll none of him!"

"Then that leaves Philip?"

Cleone whirled about.

"Whom I would not marry were he the last man in the world!"

"Luckily he is not. Don't be so violent, my dear."

Cleone stood for a moment, irresolute. Then she burst into tears and ran out of the room.

Lady Malmerstoke leaned back against the cushions and closed her eyes.

"There's hope for you yet, Philip," she remarked, and prepared to go to sleep. It was not to be. Barely five minutes later Sir Maurice was ushered into the room.

Her ladyship sat up, a hand to her wig.

"Really, Maurice, you should know better than to take a woman unawares!" she said severely. "Your family has been in and out the house all the morning. What's the matter now?"

Sir Maurice kissed her hand.

"First, my heartiest congratulations, Sarah! I have just seen Tom."

If a lady could grin, Sarah Malmerstoke grinned then.

"Thank you, Maurice. And how did you find Tom?"

"Quite incoherent," said Sir Maurice. "He has

talked a deal of nonsense about love-passions belonging only to the young, but I never saw a man so madly elated in my life."

"How nice!" sighed my lady blissfully. "And what's your second point?"

Sir Maurice walked to the fire and stared into it.

"Sally, it's Cleone."

"Dear me! What's to do?"

"If anyone can help me, it's you," he began.

Her ladyship held up her hands.

"No, Maurice, no! You're too old!"

"You ridiculous woman!" He smiled a little. "Does she care for Philip, or does she not?"

"Well"—my lady bit her finger—"I've been asking her that question, or one like it, myself."

"What did she say?"

"That she wouldn't marry him were he the last man in the world."

Sir Maurice looked at her wretchedly.

"What's come over her? I thought— She said nothing more?"

"Not a word. She burst into tears and fled."

His face brightened.

"Surely that augurs well for him?"

"Very well," nodded my lady. "But—"

"But what? Tell me, Sally!"

"You're very anxious," she observed.

"Of course I am anxious! I tell you Philip is head over ears in love with the child! And she—"

"And she," finished her ladyship deliberately, "will need a deal of convincing that it is so. We are told that Philip is in love with Ann Nutley. We know that Philip trifled elegantly with various French ladies. We see him being kind to little Jennifer. And so on."

"But he means nothing! You know that!"

"I? Does it matter what I know? It is what Cleone knows, but there's naught under the sun so unreasonable as a maid in love."

"But if Philip assures her——"

"Pho!" said her ladyship, and snapped her fingers. "Pho!"

"She wouldn't believe it?"

"She might. But she might not choose to show it."

"But it's ridiculous! It's—"

"Of course. All girls are ridiculous."

"Sally, don't be tiresome! What's to be done?"

"Leave 'em alone," counselled her ladyship. "There's no good to be got out of interfering. Philip must play his own game."

"He intends to. But he does not know whether she loves him or not!"

"You can tell him from me that there is hope, but that he must go carefully. And now I'm going to sleep. Good-bye, Maurice."

CHAPTER XVI

Mistress Cleone Finds there is No Safety in Numbers

When Philip entered the ballroom of my Lady Dering's house, on Wednesday evening, Lady Malmerstoke had already arrived. Cleone was dancing with Sir Deryk; Jennifer was sitting beside her ladyship, looking very shy and very bewildered. As soon as he could do so, Philip made his way to that end of the room.

Lady Malmerstoke welcomed him with a laugh.

"Good even, Philip! Have you brought your papa?"

Philip shook his head.

"He preferred to go to White's with Tom. Jenny, you'll dance with me, will you not? Remember, you promised!"

Jennifer raised her eyes.

"I—I doubt I—cannot. I— I have danced so few times, sir."

"Don't tell me those little feet cannot dance, *chérie!*"

Jennifer glanced down at them.

"It's monstrous kind of you, Philip—but—but are you sure you want to lead me out?"

Philip offered her his arm.

"I see you are in a very teasing mood, Jenny," he scolded.

Jennifer rose.

"Well, I will—but—oh, I am very nervous! I expect you dance so well."

"I don't think I do, but I am sure you underrate your dancing. Let us essay each other!"

From across the room Cleone saw them. She promptly looked away, but contrived, nevertheless, to keep an eye on their movements. She saw Philip presently lead Jenny to a chair and sit talking to her. Then he hailed a passing friend and presented him to Jennifer. Cleone watched him walk across the room to a knot of men. He returned to Jennifer with several of them. Unreasoning anger shook Cleone. Why did Philip care what happened to Jennifer? Why was he so assiduous in his attentions? She told herself she was an ill-natured cat, but she was still angry. From Jennifer Philip went to Ann Nutley.

Sir Deryk stopped fanning Cleone.

"There he goes! I declare, Philip Jettan makes love to every pretty woman he meets! Just look at them!"

Cleone was looking. Her little teeth were tightly clenched.

"Mr. Jettan is a flatterer," she said.

"Always so abominably French, too. Mistress Ann seems amused. I believe Jettan is a great favourite with the ladies of Paris."

Suddenly Cleone remembered that duel that Philip had fought "over the fair name of some French maid."

"Yes?" she said carelessly. "Of course, he is very handsome."

"Do you think so? Oh, here he comes! Evidently the lovely Ann does not satisfy him. . . . Your servant, sir!"

Philip smiled and bowed.

"Mademoiselle, may I have the honour of leading you out?" he asked.

Above all, she must not show Philip that she cared what he did.

"Oh, I have but this instant sat down!" she said, "I protest I am fatigued and very hot!"

"I know of a cool withdrawing-room," said Brenderby at once. "Let me take you to it, fairest!"

"It's very kind, Sir Deryk, but I do not think I will go. If I might have a glass of ratafia?" she added plaintively, looking at Philip.

For once he was backward in responding. Sir Deryk bowed.

"At once, dear lady! I go to procure it!"

"Oh, thank you, sir!" This was not what Cleone wanted at all. "Well, Mr. Jettan, you have not yet fled to Paris?"

Philip sat down beside her.

"No, mademoiselle, not yet. To-night will decide whether I go or stay." His voice was rather stern.

"Indeed? How vastly exciting!"

"Is it not! I am going to ask you a plain question, Cleone. Will you marry me?"

Cleone gasped in amazement. Unreasoning fury shook her. That Philip should dare to come to her straight from the smiles of Ann Nutley! She glanced at him. He was quite solemn. Could it be that he mocked her? She forced herself to speak lightly.

"I can hardly suppose that you are serious, sir!"

"I am in earnest, Cleone, never more so. We have played at cross-purposes long enough."

His voice sent a thrill through her. Almost he was the Philip of Little Fittledean. Cleone forced herself to remember that he was not.

"Cross-purposes, sir? I fail to understand you!"

163

"Yes? Have you ever been honest with me, Cleone?"

"Have you ever been honest with me, Mr. Jettan?" she said sharply.

"Yes, Cleone. Before you sent me away I was honest with you. When I came back, no. I wished to see whether you wanted me as I was, or as I pretended to be. You foiled me. Now I am again honest with you. I say that I love you, and I want you to be my wife."

"You say that you love me. . . ." Cleone tapped her fan on her knee. "Perhaps you will continue to be honest with me, sir. Am I the only one you have loved?"

"You are the only one."

The blue eyes flashed.

"And what of the ladies of the French Court, Mr. Jettan? What of a certain duel you fought with a French husband? You can explain that, no doubt?"

Philip was silent for a moment, frowning.

"So the news of that absurd affair reached you, Cleone?"

She laughed, clenching her teeth.

"Oh, yes, sir! It reached me. A pity, was it not?"

"A great pity, Cleone, if on that gossip you judge me."

"Ah! There was no truth in the tale?" Suppressed eagerness was in her voice.

"I will be frank with you. A certain measure of truth there was. M. de Foli-Martin thought himself injured. It was not so."

"And why should he think so, sir?"

"Presumably because I paid court to madame, his wife."

164

"Yes?" Cleone spoke gently, dangerously. "You paid court to madame. No doubt she was very lovely?"

"Very." Philip was nettled.

"As lovely, perhaps, as Mademoiselle de Marcherand, of whom I have heard, or as Mistress Ann Nutley yonder? Or as lovely as Jennifer?"

Philip took a false step.

"Cleone, surely you are not jealous of little Jenny?" he cried.

She drew herself up.

"Jealous? What right have I to be jealous? You are nothing to me, Mr. Jettan! I confess that once I—liked you. You have changed since then. You cannot deny that you have made love to a score of beautiful women since you left home. I do not blame you for that. You are free to do as you please. What I will not support is that you should come to me with your proposal, having shown me during the time that you have spent in England that I am no more to you than Ann Nutley, or Julie de Marcherand. 'To the Pearl that Trembles in Her Ear', was it not? Very pretty, sir. And now I intrigue you for the moment. I cannot consider myself flattered, Mr. Jettan."

Philip had grown pale under his paint.

"Cleone, you wrong me! It is true that I have trifled harmlessly with those ladies. It is the fashion—the fashion you bade me follow. There has never been aught serious betwixt any woman and me. That I swear!"

"You probably swore the same to M. de Foli-Martin?"

"When I gave him the satisfaction he craved, yes."

"I suppose he believed you?"

"No." Philip bit his lip.

"No? Then will you tell me, sir, how it is that you

165

expect me to believe what M. de Foli-Martin—closely concerned—would not believe?"

Philip looked straight into her eyes.

"I can only give you my word, Cleone."

Still she fought on, wishing to be defeated.

"So you have never trifled with any of these women, sir?"

Philip was silent again.

"You bring me"—Cleone's voice trembled—"a tarnished reputation. I've no mind to it, sir. You have made love to a dozen other women. Perhaps you have kissed them. And—now you offer me—your kisses! I like unspoilt wares, sir."

Philip rose, very stiff and stern.

"I am sorry that you consider yourself insulted by my offer, Cleone."

Her hand half flew towards him and fell again. Couldn't he understand that she wanted him to beat down her resistance? Did he care no more than that? If only he would deny everything and master her!

"I hasten to relieve you of my obnoxious presence. Your servant, mademoiselle." Philip bowed. He turned on his heel and walked away, leaving Cleone stricken.

Her fan dropped unheeded to the ground. Philip had gone! He had not understood that she wanted to be overruled, overcome. He had gone, and he would never come back. In those few minutes he had been the Philip she loved, not the flippant gallant of the past weeks. Tears came into Cleone's eyes. Why, why had he been so provoking? And oh, why had she let him go? She knew now beyond question that he was the only man she could ever love, or had ever loved. Now he had left her, and would go back to Paris.

Nothing mattered, she did not care what became of her once she had lost Philip.

James Winton, never far away, came to her side and sat down. Cleone greeted him mechanically and proceeded to follow out her own line of dismal thought. Through a haze of misery she heard James' voice. It sounded rather shy, and very anxious. She had not the faintest idea of what he was saying, but she felt vaguely annoyed by his persistency. Presently these words filtered through to her brain:

"Say yes, Cleone! Say yes! Oh, say yes, Cleone!"

How importunate he was! Cleone turned impatiently.

"Oh, yes, yes! What is it?"

As James had been blurting out a carefully-worded proposal of marriage, he was not flattered by this answer. He rose, hurt to the bottom of his youthful soul.

"It is evident that you have not heard a word of what I said, Cleone!"

"Oh, don't worry me, James! I've said yes. What is it? You are so persistent, and I wish to be quiet!"

James bowed.

"I will leave you, madam. I offered you my hand and my heart." With that he walked off, a picture of outraged dignity.

Cleone broke into hysterical laughter. Up came Sir Deryk.

"You seem vastly entertained, lady fair. May I share the pleasantry?"

Cleone sprang up.

"Take me away from this!" she begged. "I—I am nigh fainting from the heat! I—oh, I must be quiet! The fiddling goes through and through my head. I—oh, take me somewhere cool!"

Sir Deryk was surprised, but he did not show it.

"Why, of course, dearest! I know of a small with-drawing-room near-by. Take my arm, it's stifling in here!" He led her across the room to where a heavy curtain hung, shutting off a small, dimly-lighted apartment.

Meanwhile Philip had gone to Lady Malmerstoke's side. He sat down, frowning gloomily.

Her ladyship eyed him speculatively.

"Well?" she demanded.

Philip laughed bitterly.

"Oh, I have been rebuffed! Do I conceal it so admirably?"

"No, you do not," said her ladyship. "You must have played your cards monstrously badly. Trust a man."

"Oh, no! 'Tis merely that your niece does not love me."

"Fiddle! Don't tell me that. D'you think I'm a fool, Philip?"

"She objects, madam, to my—tarnished reputation. She was quite final."

"You thought she was quite final. Now, don't be stately, child! What happened?"

"I asked her to marry me—and she flung my wretched Paris *affaires* in my face."

"Of course, you denied everything?"

"No, I did not. How could I? There was a certain measure of tr—"

Lady Malmerstoke leant back disgustedly.

"God preserve me from young men! You admitted it?"

"No—that is, I was frank with her."

"Great heavens, Philip! Frank with a woman? God

help you, then! And what next? Did you tell Cleone not to be a fool? Did you insist that she should listen to you?"

"How could I? She—"

"You didn't. You walked off when you should have mastered her. I'll wager my best necklet she was waiting for you to assert yourself. And now she's probably miserable. Serve her right, and you too."

"But, Lady Malmerstoke—"

"Not but what I don't sympathise with the child," continued her ladyship inexorably. "Of course, she is a fool, but so are all girls. A woman of my age don't inquire too closely into a man's past—we've learned wisdom. Cleone knows that you have trifled with a dozen other women. Bless you, she don't think the worse of you for that!"

"She does! She said—"

"For goodness' sake, don't try to tell me what she said, Philip! What's that to do with it?"

"But you don't understand! Cleone said—"

"So she may have. That does not mean that she meant it, does it?" asked her ladyship in great scorn.

"*Mais*—"

"Don't start talking French at me, child, for I can't bear it! You should know by now that no woman means what she says when it's to a man."

"Oh, stop, stop! Lady Malmerstoke, you don't understand! Cleone does think the worse of me for those intrigues! She is very angry!"

"Of course she is. What do you expect?"

Philip clasped his head.

"*Mais, voyons!* Just now you said that she does *not* think the worse of me for it!"

"Who said she did? Can't one think two things at the same time?"

"But surely not two such—such contradictory things! I have never done so in my life!"

"You! You're only a man! You've not our gifts! I can tell you!" My lady spread out her fan. "Why, a woman can think of a hundred different things at once, all of them contradictory!" She nodded at him complacently.

"It's ridiculous! It's impossible! Are women's brains so—so incoherent?"

"Most of 'em," answered her ladyship. "They jump, you see."

"Jump?" Philip was thoroughly bewildered.

"Jump. From one thing to another. You'll arrive at a new thought by degrees, and you'll know how you got there. Women don't think like that. Cleone could not tell you why she thinks well and ill of you at once, but she does."

"But surely if she reasons with herself she'll see how absurd—"

"If she what?"

"Reasons. I mean—"

"You're mad," said Lady Malmerstoke with conviction. "Women don't reason. That's a man's part. Why, do you suppose that if Cleone thought as you think, and had a brain like a man's, you'd be in love with her? Of course you'd not. You'd not be able to feel your superiority over her. Don't tell me!"

"I don't feel—"

Her ladyship chuckled.

"Oh, don't you, Philip? You think that Clo is reasonable-minded, and able to care for herself, needing no master?"

"I—no, I don't!"

"That's what I say. Goodness me, how blind you

are! If you didn't consider that you had to care for Cleone and guard her from everyone else and herself, you wouldn't love her. Now don't be foolish!"

Philip laughed ruefully.

"You're a fount of wisdom, Lady Sally!"

"Well, I should be at my age. I've had experience, you see, and I never was a fool."

"Then—tell me what I am to do?"

Lady Malmerstoke wagged an impressive finger at him.

"Take that girl and shake her. Tell her you'll not be flouted. Tell her she's a little fool, and kiss her. And if she protests, go on kissing her. Dear me, what things I do say!"

"Yes, but, dear Lady Sally, how am I to kiss her when she's as cold as ice—and—and so unapproachable?"

"And why is she cold?" said her ladyship. "Tell me that!"

"Because she—thinks me naught but an elegant trifler!"

"Not a bit of it. Because you treat her gently and politely, and let her flout you. God bless my soul, women don't want gentle politeness! Not Cleone, at all events! They like a man to be brutal!"

"Brutal?"

"Well, not exactly. They like to feel he'll stand no airs and graces. Oh, they want gentleness, never fear! But they want to feel helpless. They want mastering, most of 'em. When you kiss the tips of Clo's fingers, and treat her as though you thought she was made o' porcelain, she thinks you're no man, and don't care for her."

"She cannot! She—"

"She don't know it, of course, but it's true. Be advised by me, Philip, and insist on having your way with her. Don't be finicky!"

"It's very well, but she doesn't love me!"

"Oh, drat the man!" said her ladyship. "You fatigue me! Go your own road, but don't blame me when everything goes awry. If you have made Clo miserable she'll do something mad. And now I've warned you. Oh, here is James, looking like a sulky bear! James, my good boy, I've left my handkerchief in another room. Will you fetch it for me, please? Over there, behind that curtain. Yes, shocking, isn't it? But 'twas only old Fotheringham, so you can tell your uncle, Philip."

He rose and laughed down at her.

"And will he master you, my lady?"

"Not he," said Lady Malmerstoke placidly. "I'm past the age of wanting that nonsense. Not that I ever wanted it, but I was always unusual. Be off with you!"

Philip took James by the arm.

"We are summarily dismissed! Come, Jamie, we'll find her handkerchief, and she'll smile again."

In the withdrawing-room Cleone was dicing with Sir Deryk. A very unmaidenly proceeding. She had just lost the rose at her breast to Brenderby, and he was trying to undo the pin that held it in place. Failing in that, he grasped the stem firmly, and broke off the bloom. But with the rose he had clutched a thin blue riband from which hung a locket. It snapped, and the trinket rolled on to the floor.

Cleone was already overwrought. She sprang up.

"Oh, my locket!" And searched wildly on the floor.

Surprised at her earnestness, Brenderby went down on his knees, and presently retrieved the locket just as

172

Cleone had seen it. He rose, and was about to present it to her when she clasped agitated hands and demanded that it should be given her at once! This aroused Sir Deryk's curiosity. He withheld it.

"Why so anxious, Cleone? What secret does it hide?"

"Naught! Oh, give it me, give it me!"

Sir Deryk held fast to the trophy.

"Not so fast, Cleone! I'll swear there's some mystery here! I've a mind to peep inside!"

"I forbid you!" said Cleone. "Sir Deryk—" She controlled herself. "Please give it me!"

"And so I will, fairest, but first I must see what is inside!"

"Oh, no, no! There's naught! I could not bear you to look! Besides, it's—it's empty. I—oh, give it me!" She stamped angrily.

Brenderby's eyes were alight with impish laughter.

"I'll make a bargain, sweetest! You shall play me for it." He picked up the dice-box: "If you beat my throw, I will give you the locket unopened. If you lose you shall pay a price for it."

"I don't understand! What do you mean?"

"You shall kiss me for it. One hard-earned kiss. Come, you must admit my terms are generous!"

"I won't! How dare you, sir! And it is *my* locket! You have no right to it!"

"What I find I keep! Come! The odds are equal, and in neither case do I open the locket."

"I—I thought you a gentleman!"

"So I am, Clo. Were I not—I'd take the price and then the locket. There's no one to see, and no one need know. Cleone—you lovely creature!"

Cleone wrung her hands.

"I should die of shame! Oh, Sir Deryk, please be kind!"

"Why should I be kind when you are not? You'll none of my terms? Very well!" He made as if to open the locket.

"No, no, no!" almost shrieked Cleone. "I'll do anything, anything! Only don't open it!"

"You'll play me?"

Cleone drew a deep breath.

"Yes. I will. And I'll never, never, never speak to you again!"

He laughed.

"Oh, I trust you'll change your mind! Now!" He cast the dice. "Aha! Can you beat that?"

Cleone took the box in a firm clasp, and shook it long and violently. Her cheeks were burning, her eyes tight shut. She threw the dice. Brenderby bent over the table.

"Alack!"

Her eyes flew open.

"I've won? Oh, I have won!"

"No. I was grieving for you, fairest, not for myself. You have lost."

Tears glistened on the end of her long lashes.

"Sir Deryk—p-please be gen-generous now! I don't want to—kiss you!"

"What! You cry off? Shame, Cleone!" he teased.

"You are monstrous unk-kind! It's my locket, and I d-don't want to kiss you! I don't, I don't! I hate you!"

"That adds spice, my dear. Must I take the price?"

She choked down a sob.

"Very well. Kiss me." She stood where she was, face upturned, with the resignation of a martyr.

He laid his hands on her shoulders, looking down at her.

"By God, Cleone, you're damnably beautiful!" he said thickly. "You've played with fire to-night—but I won't burn you too much!" He bent his head till his lips met hers.

At that inauspicious moment James and Philip walked into the room.

"No, it was here she said, Philip. I re—"

With a cry of horror Cleone sprang away from Sir Deryk, her cheeks flaming. Her wide eyes went from James' face of frozen astonishment to Philip's pale, furious countenance.

Philip took a half-step forward, his hand wrenching at his sword-hilt. Then he checked and slammed the sword back into the scabbard. Cleone had not struggled in Brenderby's embrace. What could he do? He had always thought her in love with the fellow. And on the top of his own proposal. . . . He swept a magnificent bow.

"*Mille pardons, mademoiselle!* It seems that I intrude."

Cleone winced at the biting sarcasm in his voice. She tried to speak, and failed. What could she say?

James came out of his stupor. He strode forward.

"What in thunder—"

"I don't kn-know!" quavered Cleone. "Oh—oh, heaven!"

Quickly Brenderby stepped to her side. He took her hand in his, and gave it a reassuring squeeze.

"Gentlemen, you have the honour of addressing my affianced wife," he said haughtily.

Philip's hand was on the curtain. It clenched slowly. He stood very still, his eyes on Cleone's face.

"Oh!" cried Cleone. "Oh, I—" She stopped helplessly. Heavens, what a position she was in! If she denied that she was betrothed to Brenderby, what could

Philip think? What must he think? He had seen her in Sir Deryk's arms; the only excuse was a betrothal. And she had accused Philip of loose behaviour! Whatever happened, he must not think her a light woman! But, oh! how could she say she was betrothed to another when she desired nothing better than to fly to him for protection? She compromised.

"I—oh, I think I am about—to faint!" she said.

Sir Deryk drew her hand through his arm.

"No, no, my love! Tell these gentlemen that it is as I say."

Cleone looked at Philip. Was he sneering? She couldn't bear it.

"Yes," she said. "It is."

Philip seemed to stiffen. He bowed again.

"Permit me to offer my felicitations," he said, but his voice was not quite steady.

James hurried forward, furious.

"Your pardon, sir! I beg leave to contradict that statement!"

They all stared at him in amazement. Philip eyed him through his quizzing-glass.

"I—beg—your—pardon?" drawled Brenderby.

"I am betrothed to her myself!" shouted James.

Cleone's hands flew to her cheeks.

"Oh!" she fluttered. "Oh—oh, I am going to faint!"

Brenderby's eyes twinkled.

"Bear up a little longer, dear! Of course, I know there is no truth in what Mr. Winton says!"

"It is true!" James danced in his fury. "Cleone promised to wed me, only a little while back! You can't deny it, Clo! You did!"

"I did not!"

"You did! You said yes! You know you did!"

Cleone leant on the nearest thing to her for support. It chanced to be Sir Deryk, but she was past caring.

"James, you know I—never meant it!"

Suddenly Philip's lips twitched. Brenderby was bubbling over with ill-suppressed merriment.

"My dear, this is most serious! Did you, indeed, accept Mr. Winton's proposal?"

"Yes, but he knows I did not mean it! I—"

"Cleone, did you tell me you accepted him and—"

"Yes, she did! And I hold her to her promise!"

Cleone's knees threatened to give way.

"James, I can't marry you! I won't marry you!"

"I hold you to your promise!" repeated James, almost beside himself.

"And I." Sir Deryk passed his arm round Cleone's waist. "I hold Cleone to the promise she has given me!"

Philip interposed.

"Probably the lady would be glad of a chair," he suggested evenly. "James, Brenderby—let your future wife sit down!"

Sir Deryk's shoulders shook. He led Cleone to the couch, and she sank on to it, hiding her face.

Philip swung the curtain aside.

"Permit me to withdraw. Decidedly I am *de trop*. Mademoiselle, messieurs!" He went out, and the curtain fell back into place.

"Oh, oh, oh!" moaned Cleone.

James bent over her.

"Come, Clo! Let me take you back to your aunt!"

Brenderby stepped to Cleone's other side.

"Cleone needs no other escort than that of her affianced husband, sir!"

"And that is I!"

"On the contrary, it is I! Cleone, sweet, come!"

Cleone sprang up.

"It's neither of you! Don't—touch me! Oh, that I should be so humiliated! I will not marry you, James! You know that I never heard what you said!"

James set his chin stubbornly.

"I'll not release you from your promise," he said.

"And nor will I." Sir Deryk was enjoying himself.

"You must release me, James!" cried Cleone. "I—I am going to wed—Sir Deryk!" She dissolved into tears. "Oh, what shall I do? What shall I do? How—how dreadful it is! Let me go! I hate you both!" She fled from them and was at her aunt's side before either had time to follow her.

"Good gracious, child, what's amiss?" exclaimed Lady Malmerstoke. "You're as white as my wig!"

"Take me home!" begged Cleone. "I am b-be-trothed to Sir Deryk and James! Oh, for heaven's sake, take me home!"

CHAPTER XVII

Mistress Cleone at her Wits' End

Sir Maurice and his brother were sitting at breakfast next morning when Philip burst in on them. Tom jumped up and swore.

"Damn you, Philip! At this hour!"

Philip paid not the slightest heed to him. He grasped his father by the shoulder.

"Father, you must to Lady Malmerstoke's house at once!"

Sir Maurice ate another mouthful of beef.

"Sit down, my son, and be calm. What's to do?"

"God alone knows!" cried Philip. He sank into a chair and rejected his uncle's offer of breakfast. "Breakfast? What have I to do with food when I'm nigh demented?"

"Drink's the thing," agreed Tom placidly. He pushed a tankard of ale towards his nephew. "What ails you, lad?"

"Cleone's betrothed to Brenderby," announced Philip wretchedly.

"No!" Tom was dumbfounded.

"And to Winton." Philip sought to drown his troubles in the tankard.

"What!" Sir Maurice dropped his knife. "Betrothed to Brenderby *and* Winton? You're raving!"

"Would to God I were!" Philip emerged from the

tankard, and wiped his lips with his father's napkin. "I asked her to marry me at the ball last night. She refused; I won't tell you her exact words. Half an hour later I found her kissing *ce scélérat* Brenderby in a secluded corner!" He laughed savagely.

"You mean that Brenderby kissed her?" suggested Tom.

"No, I do not! *Voyons*, would he be alive now had he dared embrace Cleone against her will? She submitted—she wished it!"

"I'll not believe that!" exclaimed Sir Maurice.

"You must believe it. She is betrothed to him. She said it herself. James was with me. He interposed, saying that she was already promised to him."

Tom gave a chuckle.

"Faith, the child is rich in—" He caught Philip's eye and subsided. "Oh, ay, ay! Go on."

"I know no more. I deemed it time for me to withdraw."

"The proper thing to have done," said Tom solemnly, "was to have struck an attitude and said, 'Not so! The girl is mine!'"

"What right had I? I was not amongst the favoured ones."

"Don't sneer, Philip," interposed Sir Maurice. "There must be something behind all this."

Philip turned to him.

"That's what I hope and trust! You must go at once to Lady Malmerstoke's!" His head sank into his hands and he gave way to a gust of laughter. "Oh, Gad! neither would give way an inch. Both held Clo to her promise!"

"Ye seem monstrous light-hearted about it," said his uncle.

Philip sprang up.

"Because I thought that—for one moment—she looked at me for help!"

"Which you declined to give?" asked Sir Maurice dryly.

"*Mon cher père*, I have my own game to play. Now go to Lady Malmerstoke's, I implore you!"

Sir Maurice rose.

"I'll go at once. What madness can have seized Cleone?"

Philip almost pushed him out of the room.

"That is what I want to know. Quickly, Father!"

The little black page swung open the door of my lady's boudoir.

"Sah Maurice Jettan!"

"The very man I wish to see!" exclaimed Lady Malmerstoke. "Maurry, never were you more opportune!"

Sir Maurice kissed her hand with punctilious politeness. He then smiled at Cleone, who stood by the table, pale and wan-looking.

"I hope I see you well, Cleone?"

"Very well, thank you, sir," said Cleone dully.

Lady Malmerstoke sat down.

"Clo has disgraced me," she said comfortably. "Is it not exciting?"

Cleone turned her head away. Sir Maurice saw her lips tremble.

"Please, Aunt—please don't—don't—I shall wed—Sir Deryk."

"And what's to happen to t'other? You can't wed two men, my dear. I'm not sure that I shall consent to your marrying either."

"Sir Deryk—has my word."

"But so has James."

"What's this?" Sir Maurice spoke with well-feigned

181

astonishment. "Cleone, you are not betrothed, surely?"

"To two men," nodded her aunt. "I have never been so amused in my life. I always considered myself to be flighty, but I'll swear I never was engaged to two men at one and the same time!"

Cleone sat down, staring out of the window and biting her lips.

"What!" cried Sir Maurice in liveliest horror. "Engaged to two men? Cleone!"

The golden head was bowed. A great sob shook Cleone.

"But—good heavens, my dear! This is dreadful! How could such a thing have come to pass?"

"Of course it's dreadful," said her ladyship. "Think of the scandal when it is known. And that'll be soon, I'll wager. Brenderby will never keep such a piece of spice to himself." As she spoke, one of her eyelids flickered. Sir Maurice smiled, unseen by Cleone.

"You—forget, Aunt. I am going to—wed—Sir Deryk." A shudder ran through her at the thought.

"But I don't understand! Tell me how it happened, Cleone!"

"Yes, tell him, Clo. Mayhap he can help you."

"No one can help me," said Cleone miserably. "I must bear the pain of my own folly. I—oh, I have been so wicked!"

"Now, Cleone? Why? What happened?"

"I may as well tell you. It will be all over town by to-night—everyone will know me for a flirtatious, flighty woman. I—"

"You won't have a shred of reputation left," said her aunt maliciously.

Cleone started.

"Rep— Oh, and I said—!"

182

"Said what, my love?"

"Naught. I—I—oh, Sir Maurice, Sir Maurice, I am so unhappy!" Cleone burst into tears.

Sir Maurice patted one heaving shoulder.

"There, there, Cleone! Tell me all about it!"

"It—it was at the ball last n-night. I—I—no, first James proposed—to me, and I said yes, but I didn't mean it!"

"You said yes, but you didn't mean it?"

"I didn't hear what he said—I—I said yes because he worried so! And—and he knew I didn't mean it, for he walked away. Then I—I—went with Sir Deryk to a room apart—"

"Cle-one!"

"Oh, I know, I know! It was terrible of me, but I was so upset—I—I hardly cared what I did!"

"But why were you upset? Because James had proposed?"

"No—I—I—something—else—I can't tell you! Anyway—Sir Deryk took me to this room, and—and taught me to—to dice—yes, I know it was horrid! And —and I lost my rose to him, and when he—was taking it, he broke the string of my locket, and he wouldn't give it me, but said he must see what was inside, and I *couldn't* let him! I *couldn't!*"

"What was inside?" asked Sir Maurice.

"For heaven's sake, don't ask her that!" begged Lady Malmerstoke. "It sets her off into floods of tears!"

"Aunt, *please!* And—and so I played him—for it— and I lost and had to—to kiss him—for it. Don't, don't look at me! And then—and then *he* came—with James —and saw! What he must *think* of me! And I said that he— Oh, he must—"

"Who is 'he'?" asked Sir Maurice innocently. He watched a tell-tale blush steal up under Cleone's fingers.

"Mr.—Mr. Jettan—I—he—saw me kiss—Sir Deryk! Then—then—I think, to spare me—Sir Deryk said I was his betrothed wife. I could not say I was not, could I? It was too dreadful! And Phil—Mr. Jettan congratulated us! But James suddenly said *he* was going to marry me because I had said yes to him—by mistake! Of course I said I was not, but he wouldn't release me from my word, and nor would Sir Deryk! Then—then he—Ph—I mean Mr. Jettan—just bowed and went away, but I could see what he—thought of —of me. Oh, what shall I do? Neither will let me go! I am betrothed to two gentlemen, and—oh, *what* shall I do?"

Sir Maurice took a pinch of snuff. A smile hovered about his mouth. He shut the box with a snap.

"It seems, my dear, that the situation calls for a third gentleman," he said, and picked up his hat.

Cleone sprang to her feet.

"Oh—oh, what are you going to do?" she cried.

Sir Maurice walked to the door.

"It needs a masterful hand to extricate you from your delicate position," he said. "I go in search of such a hand."

Cleone ran to him, clasping his arm.

"No, no, no! Oh, for heaven's sake, Sir Maurice, stop!"

He laid a hand over her clutching fingers.

"My dear, do you want a scandal?"

"No, oh no! But I must persuade James!"

"And do you want to marry this Brenderby?"

"I—am going to marry him."

"Cleone, answer me! Do you want to marry him?"

184

"I don't want to marry anyone! I wish I were dead!"

"Well, child, you are not dead. I refuse to see you fall into Brenderby's clutches, and I refuse to countenance the scandal that would arise if you rejected him. I am too old to serve you, but I know of one who is not."

"Sir Maurice, I implore you, do not speak to him! You don't understand!— Oh, stop, stop!"

Sir Maurice had disengaged himself. He opened the door.

"You need not fear that the third gentleman will cause you any annoyance, my dear. I can vouch for his discretion."

Cleone tried to hold him back.

"Sir Maurice, you don't understand! You must not ask Ph—your son to—to—help me! I—I didn't tell you all! I— Oh, come back!"

The door closed behind Sir Maurice.

"A very prompt, wise man," commented Lady Malmerstoke. "Now I am to be baulked of the scandal. Hey-dey!"

Cleone paced to and fro.

"I can't face him! I can't, I can't! What must he *think* of me! What must he think? Aunt, you don't know all!"

"Oh, yes, I do," retorted her ladyship.

"No, no, you do not! Philip asked me to marry him —and I refused! I—I—told him—I would not marry a man with a tarnished reputation! I—I said that—and worse! I accused him of trifling and—and—oh, it's too awful! That he should have been the one to see! How he must scorn me. Oh, Aunt, Aunt, can't you say something?"

"Ay, one thing. That you will have to be very humble to Master Philip. At least, he was never betrothed twice in one night."

Cleone collapsed on to the couch.

"I'll not see him! I—oh, I must go home at once! I must, I must! Everything is all my fault! I ought never to have—sent him away! And now—and now he despises me!"

"Who says so?"

"I—how could he do else? Don't—don't you realise how dreadful I have been? And—and his face—when —when he—heard everything! He'll never never believe—the truth!"

"What matters it?" asked my lady carelessly. "Since you do not love him—"

"Oh, I do, I do, I do!" wept Cleone.

François admitted Sir Maurice. His round face was perturbed. It cleared somewhat at the sight of Sir Maurice.

"Ah, m'sieur, *entrez donc!* M'sieur Philippe he is like one mad!—He rage, he go up and down the room like a caged beast! It is a woman, without doubt it is a woman! I have known it *depuis longtemps!* Something terrible has happened! M'sieur is *hors de lui-même!*"

Sir Maurice laughed.

"Poor François! I go to reassure m'sieur."

"Ah, if m'sieur can do that!"

"I can—most effectively. Where is he?"

François pointed to the library door.

Philip literally pounced on his father.

"Well? You have seen her? Is she in love with Brenderby? Is she to wed him? What did she tell you?"

186

Sir Maurice pushed him away.

"You are the second distracted lover who has clutched me to-day. Have done."

Philip danced with impatience.

"But speak, Father! Speak!"

Sir Maurice sat down leisurely and crossed his legs.

"At the present moment Cleone is betrothed. Very much so," he added, chuckling. "I am about to put the whole matter into your hands."

"My hands? She wants my help?"

"Not at all. She is insistent that you shall not be appealed to. In fact, she was almost frantic when I suggested it."

"Then does she not want to marry Brenderby?"

"Certainly not. But she will do so if you fail to intervene."

Philip flung out his hands.

"But tell me, sir! What happened last night?"

"Sit down and be quiet," said Sir Maurice severely. "I am on the point of telling you."

Philip obeyed meekly.

"And don't interrupt." Sir Maurice proceeded to relate all that he had heard from Cleone. . . . "And she was so upset that she went with Brenderby, not caring what happened. That is the whole story," he ended.

"Upset? But—was she upset—because I had offered and been rejected?"

"Presumably. Now she is so hopelessly compromised that she daren't face you."

Philip sank his head into his hands and gave way to a long peal of laughter.

"*Sacré nom de Dieu,* the tables are turned, indeed. Oh, Clo, Clo, you wicked little hussy! And what was in that locket?"

"That you will have to ask her yourself," answered Sir Maurice.

Philip jumped up.

"And I shall. *Mordieu*, never did I dream of such a solution to my difficulties!"

"Perhaps she still will not have you, Philip," warned Sir Maurice.

Philip flung back his head.

"Thunder of God, she will have me now if I have to force her to the altar! *Ciel*, you have taken a load off my mind, sir! I thought she cared for Brenderby! She smiled on him so consistently. And now for *ce cher* Brenderby! I am going to enjoy myself."

"Remember, Philip! No breath of scandal!"

"Am I so clumsy? Not a whisper shall there be! François, François! My hat, my cloak, my boots, and my SWORD!"

CHAPTER XVIII

Philip Takes Charge of the Situation

Sir Deryk's valet came to him, bowing.

"There is a gentleman below who desires speech with you, sir."

"Oh? Who is he?"

"Mr. Philip Jettan, sir."

Sir Deryk raised his eyebrows.

"Jettan? What can he want with me? Ay, I'll come." He rose and went languidly downstairs. "This is an unexpected honour, Jettan! Come in!" He led Philip into a large room. "Is it a mere friendly visit?"

"Anything but that," said Philip. "I have come to tell you that you will not be able to wed Mistress Cleone Charteris."

"Oh?" Brenderby laughed. "Why do you say that?"

"Because," Philip smiled a little, "I am going to wed her myself."

"You? Oh, Gad, you make the third!"

"And there is, as you know, luck in odd numbers. Are you satisfied?"

"Satisfied? Damme, no! The girl's lovely! I've a mind to her."

"Even though I tell you that she desires to be released?"

"Even though she told it me herself!"

189

"I trust you will allow me to persuade you?" Philip patted his sword-hilt lovingly.

A light sprang to Brenderby's eyes.

"Is it a fight you're wanting? By Gad, no man has ever had need to challenge me twice! Here? Now? Help me push the table back!"

"One moment! You love a hazard, I think? I fight you for the right to wed Mistress Cleone. If I win you relinquish all claim upon her, and you swear never to breathe a word of what passed last night. If you win —oh, if you win, you do as you please!"

"Ay, aught you will! I've been pining for a fight for many a long day. You're a man after my heart, stap me if you're not! Here, wait while I fetch my sword!" He hurried out of the room, returning in a very short time with a rapier. "I've told my man that you have come to fence with me. But we'll lock the door in case of accidents. How does my sword measure with yours?"

Philip compared them.

"Very well." His eyes danced suddenly. "*Dieu!* I never thought to fight so strange a duel!" He pulled off his boots. "We'll fight in wigs, yes? One is so displeasing without a hair to one's head."

"A dozen, if you like!" Brenderby struggled out of his coat and vest. "You know, you are shorter than I am. We're not fair matched."

Philip laughed, tucking up his ruffles.

"No matter. You see, I must win!"

"Why?" Brenderby made an imaginary pass in the air.

"So much depends on it," explained Philip. "Is the light fair to both?"

"Fair enough," said Brenderby.

"You are ready, then? *Eh bien!*"

The blades met and hissed together.

Opening in quarte, Brenderby seemed at first to be the better of the two. Philip stayed on the defensive, parrying deftly and allowing Brenderby to expend his energies. Once Brenderby's blade flashed out and all but pinked Philip, but he managed to recover his opposition in time. His eyes opened wider; he became more cautious. Suddenly he descried an opening and lunged forward. There was a moment's scuffle, and Brenderby put the murderous point aside. Then Philip seemed to quicken. When Brenderby began to pant, Philip changed his tactics, and gave back thrust for thrust. His wrist was like flexible steel; his footwork was superb; the whole style of his fencing was different from that of Brenderby.

All at once Brenderby saw an opening. He thrust in quinte, steel scraped against steel, and Philip's point flashed into his right arm above the elbow.

Brenderby staggered back, clutched at his arm, and tried to raise his sword again. But Philip was at his side, supporting him.

"It's only a flesh wound—painful now—*bien sûr*. It will—heal quickly. I do not—mistake," he gasped.

"Damme—I'm not done for—yet!"

"But yes! I fight—no more. You cannot—keep your blade—steady—now! Sit down!" He lowered Brenderby into a chair, and whisked out his handkerchief. He bound up Sir Deryk's wound and fetched him a glass of wine from a decanter on the sideboard.

"Thanks!" Sir Deryk gulped it down. "But where are my manners? Pour some for yourself, Jettan! Gad, but you pinked me neatly!" He seemed to slip back into his habitual drawl. "As pretty a piece of

191

sword-play as I wish to see. But you fence French-fashion."

Philip drank some wine.

"Yes. It was at Paris that I learned. With Guillaume Corvoisier."

"No!" Brenderby heaved himself up. "Corvoisier, forsooth! No wonder you're so quick!"

Philip smiled and bowed.

"You frightened me more than once, sir."

"Faith, it wasn't apparent then! You were so intent on winning?"

"It means so much, you see," said Philip simply. "My whole life's happiness."

"What! You really intend to wed Cleone?"

Again Philip bowed.

"I have always intended to wed her."

"You?" Brenderby stared. "I never knew that! What of that young sprig Winton?"

"Oh, I think I can persuade James!"

"Like this?" Brenderby glanced down at his arm.

"No, not like that. Tell me, sir, did you intend to wed mademoiselle?"

"Heaven forbid! I've no mind to tie myself up yet awhile. Your entrance last night forced me to say what I did to spare the lady's blushes. I'd no notion of continuing the comedy, until young Winton thrust in with his prior claim. Gad, but 'twas amusing! Did you not find it so?"

"I? No. But I was closely concerned in the affair, you see. I may take it that you will say naught of last night's work?"

"Of course not. 'Twas a mad jest, but I'd not let it go so far as to damage a lady's reputation. And you

192

may tell Mistress Cleone that I apologise—for what happened before. She's too damnably beautiful."

Philip worked himself into his coat.

"'Damnably' is not the word I should employ, but *n'importe*." He sat down and started to pull on his boots. "I have enjoyed myself. I said I should."

"Tare an' 'ounds, so have I! It's an age since I've had a sword in my hand. I am indebted to you, sir."

"Yes, you are out of practice. I thank the kind fates for that!"

"Ay, I'd have kept you at it longer, but I don't know that the issue would have been different. You must go?"

Philip picked up his hat.

"I must. I have to thank you for—"

"Oh, stuff! I'd no notion of holding Cleone to her promise, but I could not resist the offer of a fight. I wish you could see how monstrous amusing it was, though!"

Philip laughed.

"Had it been anyone but Cleone I might have been able to appreciate the humour of the situation! I trust the wound will heal quickly."

"Oh, that's naught! A mere prick, but I was winded. Fare ye well, Jettan. My felicitations! You felicitated me last night, did you not?" He laughed.

"With black murder in my heart!" nodded Philip. "I do not say good-bye, but *au revoir*!"

"Here's my hand on it then—my left hand, alack!"

Philip grasped it. Brenderby accompanied him to the front door and waved to him as he ran down the steps.

"*Bonne chance*, as you'd say yourself! *Au 'voir*!"

Philip waved back at him and turned to hail a pass-

193

ing chair. He instructed the bearers to carry him to Jermyn Street.

It seemed that the luck was indeed with him, for he arrived just as James was descending the steps of his house. Philip sprang out, paid the chairmen, and took Winton's arm.

"My friend, a word with you!"

"Yes?" said James. "You seem excited, Philip."

"It's what I am, then. I've come to speak to you of Cleone."

James stiffened.

"I'll not give her up to that fellow Brenderby!" he said fiercely. "It's more than flesh and blood can bear."

"Assuredly. But will you give her up to me?"

James turned to stare at him.

"You? But she is to wed Brenderby!"

"Ah, but no! that is at an end. Brenderby releases her. He is not so bad a man as you think. *En effet,* I like him."

"I loathe the sight of him, drawling fop!"

"To-day I have seen him in another light. But that is not what I have to say. Cleone does not wish to marry you, *mon enfant,* and it is churlish to persist."

"I know she'll never marry me," answered James gloomily. "I only held her to her word because I thought she'd have Brenderby if I did not."

"I understand. You'll release her—for me?"

"I suppose so. Why did you say naught last night?"

"There were reasons. They no longer exist. Come, Jamie, don't look so glum! You are young yet."

"It's easy to say that. Oh, I knew I never had a chance with her! I congratulate you, Philip."

Philip pressed his arm.

194

"My thanks. You're very generous, and now I must fly!"

"Where? May I accompany you?"

"Again many thanks, but no! I have an engagement. *Au revoir, mon cher!*"

CHAPTER XIX

Philip Justifies his Chin

Once more Lady Malmerstoke's page went up to the boudoir.

"Mistah Philip Jettan is below, m'lady!"

Up started Cleone.

"I will not see him! Aunt Sarah, I beg you will go to him! Please spare me this—humiliation!"

Lady Malmerstoke waved her aside.

"Admit him, Sambo. Yes, here. Cleone, control yourself!"

"I can't see him! I can't! I can't! How *can* I face him?"

"Turn your back, then," said her unsympathetic aunt. "I wonder what he has done?"

"D-do you think he—could have—arranged everything?" asked Cleone, with a gleam of hope.

"From what I have seen of him, I should say yes. A masterful young man, my dear. Else why that chin?" She moved to the door. Philip came in, immaculate as ever. "Ah, Philip!"

Philip shot a look past her. Cleone had fled to the window. He bent and kissed Lady Malmerstoke's hand.

"*Bonjour*, madame!" He held open the door and bowed.

Her ladyship laughed.

"What! Turning me from my own boudoir?"

"If you please, madame."

"Aunt—Sarah!" The whisper came from the window.

Philip smiled faintly.

"Madame . . ."

"Oh, that chin!" said her ladyship, and patted it. She went out and Philip closed the door behind her.

Cleone's fingers clasped one another desperately. Her heart seemed to have jumped into her throat. It almost choked her. She dared not look round. She heard the rustle of Philip's coat-skirts. Never, never had she felt so ashamed, or so frightened.

"Your devoted servant, mademoiselle!"

Cleone could not speak. She stood where she was, trembling uncontrollably.

"I have the honour of informing you, mademoiselle, that you are released from your engagements."

Was there a note of laughter in the prim voice?

"I—thank you—sir," whispered Cleone. Her teeth clenched in an effort to keep back the tears. She was blinded by them, and her bosom was heaving.

There was a slight pause. Why did he not go? Did he wish to see her still more humiliated?

"I have also to offer, on Sir Deryk's behalf, his apologies for the happenings of last night, mademoiselle."

"Th-thank—you, sir."

Again the nerve-killing silence. If only he would go before she broke down!

"Cleone . . ." said Philip gently.

The tears were running down her cheeks, but she kept her head turned away.

"Please—go!" she begged huskily.

He was coming across the room towards her. . . .

Cleone gripped her hands.

"Cleone . . . dearest!"

A heartbroken sob betrayed her. Philip took her in his arms.

"My sweetheart! Crying? Oh no, no! There is naught now to distress you."

The feel of his arms about her was sheer bliss; their strength was like a haven of refuge. Yet Cleone tried to thrust him away.

"What—must you—think of me!" she sobbed.

He drew her closer, till her head rested against his shoulder.

"Why, that you are a dear, foolish, naughty little Cleone. *Chérie*, don't cry. It is only your Philip—your own Philip, who has always loved you, and only you. Look up, my darling, look up!"

Cleone gave way to the insistence of his arms.

"Oh, Philip—forgive me!" she wept. "I have—been mad!" She raised her head and Philip's arms tightened still more. He bent over her and kissed her parted lips almost fiercely.

Later, seated beside him on the couch, her head on his shoulder, and his arm about her, Cleone gave a great sigh.

"But why—why did you treat me so—hatefully—when you—came back, Philip?"

"I was hurt, darling, and wished to see whether you wanted the real me—or a painted puppet. But then you changed suddenly—and I knew not what to think."

Cleone nestled closer.

"Because I thought you—did not care! But oh, Philip, Philip, I have been so unhappy!"

Philip promptly kissed her.

"And—last night—Philip, you don't think I—"

"Sweetheart! Is it likely that I'd believe ill of you?"

She hid her face.

"I—I believed—ill—of you," she whispered.

"But you do not believe it now, sweetheart?"

"No, oh no! But—but—that duel with Mr. Bancroft. Was it—was it—some—French lady?"

Philip was silent for a moment.

"No, Cleone. That is all I can say."

"Was it"—her voice was breathless—"was it—me?"

Philip did not answer.

"It was! How wonderful!"

Philip was startled.

"You are pleased, Cleone? Pleased?"

"Of course I am! I—oo!" She gave a little wriggle of delight. "Why did you not tell me?"

"It is not—one of the things one tells one's lady-love," said Philip.

"Oh! And to-day? How did you—persuade Sir Deryk?"

"Through the arm. But he had no intention of holding you to your word."

Cleone grew rather rigid.

"Oh—indeed? In-deed?"

Philip was mystified.

"You did not want to be held to it, did you, *chérie*?"

"No-no. But— I don't like him. Philip."

"I did not, I confess. I think I do now."

"Do you? And what of James?"

"Oh, James! He will recover."

There was a pause while Cleone digested this.

"Philip?"

"Cleone?"

"You—you—don't care for Jenny, do you?"

"Jenny? Cleone, for shame! Because I was polite—"

"More than that, Philip!"

"Well, dearest, no one paid any heed to her or was
kind. What would you?"

"It was only that? I thought—I thought—"

"Cleone, you think too much," he chid her. "Next
you will accuse me of loving Ann Nutley!" It was a
master-stroke, and he knew it.

"You didn't? Not a tiny bit?"

"Not an atom!"

"And no one—in Paris?"

"No one. I have pretended, but they all knew that I
had already lost my heart."

"You pretended . . . ? Oh!"

"One must, sweetest."

"But—"

He drew her closer.

"But never, most beautiful, did I become engaged
—twice in one evening!" He stifled the cry that rose to
her lips.

"Philip, that is ungallant, and—and hateful!"

He laughed.

"Is it not? Ah, Cleone! Tell me, my dearest, what is
in your locket?"

"Something I meant to burn," she murmured.

"But did not?"

"No—I could not." She fumbled at her bosom and
drew out the trinket. "See for yourself, Philip."

He opened it. A rolled lock of brown hair fell out
and a torn scrap of parchment. Philip turned it over.

"Yours till death, Philip," he read. "Cleone, my
love."

She buried her face on his shoulder.

"Your—hair—your poor hair!" she said.

"All gone! Look up, Cleone!"

She lifted her face. He gazed down at her, rapt.

"Oh, Cleone—I shall write a sonnet to your wonderful eyes!" he breathed.